The Lords of Lawlessness

In four brutal decades, they climbed from the depths of the New York slums to the heights of influence in the shadow of the White House itself.

There was no crime they wouldn't commit to get where they wanted, what they wanted, or whom they wanted.

No crime, that is, but one.

Then that last taboo was broken—an allies became enemies in a to-the-death struggle that turned their underworld empire into a bloody battleground where nothing was sacred. . . .

ONCE UPON A TIME IN AMERICA

The Best in Fiction from SIGNET

ONCE UPON A TIME IN AMERICA

Lee Hays

A SIGNET BOOK

NEW AMERICAN LIBRARY

NAL BOOKS ARE AVAILABLE AT QUANTITY DISCOUNTS WHEN USED TO PROMOTE PRODUCTS OR SERVICES. FOR INFORMATION PLEASE WRITE TO PREMIUM MARKETING DIVISION, NEW AMERICAN LIBRARY, 1633 BROADWAY, NEW YORK, NEW YORK 10019.

This work is a novelization of the screenplay for *Once Upon a Time in America*, written by Sergio Leone, Leonardo Benvenuti, Piero De Bernardi, Enrico Medioli, Franco Arcalli, and Franco Ferrini. The screenplay was based on the novel *The Hoods* by Harry Grey.

SIGNET TRADEMARK REG. U.S. PAT. OFF. AND FOREIGN COUNTRIES
REGISTERED TRADEMARK—MARCA REGISTRADA
HECHO EN CHICAGO, U.S.A.

SIGNET, SIGNET CLASSIC, MENTOR, PLUME, MERIDIAN AND NAL BOOKS are published by
New American Library,
1633 Broadway,
New York, New York 10019

First Printing, June, 1984

1 2 3 4 5 6 7 8 9

PRINTED IN THE UNITED STATES OF AMERICA

Bells, drums, and xylophone, the music of the gamelan, filled the air, clashed harmonically as well as culturally with the voices from the street. The voices, too, were at odds, in this case with one another, as they sang in several keys and with varying degrees of irony. "God Bless America" was the song, and Prohibition had officially come to an end on this day of 1933, and many members of the motley chorus were praising the deity—drunkenly, but with sincerity—for relief from that burden. But, it was also the Depression, and a good many of the singers were without income, which accounted for the hint of mockery in their rendition of the lyric.

Inside, the twelve-toned Far Eastern music kept fitful time with the shadows taking shape on the screen at the front of the room. The audience comprised a few scattered spectators, most of them half-asleep, several engaged in various forms of sexual congress, none of them truly interested in the ancient ritual being enacted before them, the age-old conflict between Good and Evil. The shadowy figures on the screen, bowing and dancing at the whim of the clever puppeteer, seemed to be ghostly inhabitants of another world, demons not from another continent but from far beneath the earth, hellish in shape as well as action. As the viewers dozed or found brief unrewarding ecstasy, the screen clouded over as a huge bat spread its wings to permanently crowd out the light and envelop all who were foolish enough to come within its grasp.

CHAPTER
1

1933

The hotel room across the street was dark. The dim illumination from the thirty-watt bulb in the corridor was barely strong enough to cast a pale shadow as the girl opened the door and fumbled for the light switch on the wall. Expecting it to work, Eve had already closed the door behind her when the flick of the switch produced nothing. Already frightened, she stopped short, wondering if she should leave, but exhaustion urged her forward, and she carefully made her way to the night table by the head of her bed. She felt for the lamp switch, but again she was rewarded by nothing more than a hollow click. She slid her hand up the shaft of the lamp until she reached the bulb, which she tightened. At once there was light, and startled, she stepped back, her eyes riveted on the face of a twenty-five-year-old woman who had seen far too much of the world. The face was her own.

From the street she could hear discordant voices, in dragging tempo, shouting out the anthem:

> Through the night
> With a light from above ...

Suddenly, seconds after having twisted it, it dawned on her that the light bulb had been warm. Her anxiety mounting, Eve turned around and looked at the bed. The sheets, blanket, and pillow were wadded together in a big lump. Nervously she began to attempt to straighten them. Horrified, she saw the figure of a man outlined in the bedding, outlined by what looked to be bullet holes.

There was a noise, as though glass were being ground beneath the heel of a shoe, and she opened her mouth to scream, but no sound came out. As if from nowhere, four men materialized beside her, surrounding her, blocking doors and window. A blast of cold air moved the curtains, sending a chill shuddering through her entire body. The men eyed her blankly, looking at her as though she were nothing but a piece of meat on a rack. It was a look she'd seen often enough in her profession.

One of them, a short, heavyset man, held a gun in his hand. He reached down to retrieve a picture frame from the floor. The frame's glass was broken, and the jagged edges revealed the image of a man, a young man, a man she loved whom she now was expected to betray.

The heavyset man held up the frame and pointed at it with his gun.

"Where's he hiding?"

The question was matter-of-fact, the man's expression unemotional. It was then Eve knew that she had no chance, that she would soon be dead. She could only hope that it would be over quickly and would not be too painful.

"I don't know. Honest, I don't. I've been looking for him since yesterday."

"Lying bitch!" Another of the thugs stepped forward and lashed out with a vicious, accurate left hook that caught her full in the face, breaking her nose and sending her sprawling onto the bed. Her eyes pleading,

Eve brought her hand to her face and tried to stanch the blood that gushed from her nose.

From the corner of her eye she saw the man nearest the bathroom door take something from his pocket that he screwed onto the muzzle of his gun. The first man spoke again, in a tone that was almost gentle.

"Eve. Save yourself some grief. Where is he?"

"Honest to God, I don't know. I don't. Believe me." She swallowed hard, choking on the blood in her throat. "What are . . . you . . ." The words wouldn't come. "Believe me," she sobbed.

The man said, "I believe you."

"What . . . what are you gonna do to him?"

The thug nodded. The man by the bathroom raised his gun and pointed it at her. She could see the long silencer as it swung toward her, then nothing but a small hole in the center of a piece of shiny metal no bigger than a quarter pointed at her chest.

"This." She saw only the first kick of the gun; she heard nothing, for she was dead before the muted sound could reach her ears, dead before the second and third slugs reached her body, which twisted in spasm and then fell back.

The man reached over to extinguish the

lamp. Turning to the fourth man, who stood by the window, he said, "You wait here . . . in case he shows up."

He nodded toward the door and the hit man rushed to open it, pushing his gun into his coat pocket as he crossed the room. With the dim light from the hall to see by, he turned the switch on the lamp. He moved quickly across the room, and closing the door behind them, the three men left, leaving the dead and the watcher in total darkness.

In the auditorium of Chun Lao's puppet theater, oblivious to the happenings in the world outside, the audience dozed to the ancient and insinuating sound of the gamelan. Good and Evil continued their struggle, but neither triumphed, neither *could*, for then the play would be over. The shadows cast on the screen were only a fiction; still, a sense of terror permeated the building.

A tiger loomed large on the screen, engulfing a quivering, helpless rabbit. Spellbound, the aware members of the audience watched the rabbit slowly being devoured. There was no pity in their eyes.

The men who had so callously killed Eve moved unhurriedly through the narrow streets to Fat Moe's former speakeasy, legitimate for nearly twenty-four hours. It took them only seconds to gain entrance to the darkened building and to take prisoner its owner, Fat Moe himself. They tied his hands behind his back and, using the freight elevator, took him up several floors to a room that served as an office and also, on occasion, as a small gymnasium for a few of the select customers who needed to sweat out the cheap gin they had so easily purchased illegally for so many years.

In this room the men found, next to a punching bag that hung from the ceiling, a heavy hook now empty, suspended from a thick chain. They hoisted Moe onto the hook, hanging him from his arms tethered behind him, pulling the limbs up into an extremely painful position that, given his weight, in a matter of time would break them at the shoulder.

Fat Moe whimpered, but there was no other sound, no words from the hoods, who, not satisfied with seeing him dangle there, began to batter his face and body with brass knuckles, much the way would-be boxers had, earlier in the day, been battering the punching bag next to him.

Across from this spectacle, in the section of the room that served as an office, one hood sat in a deep leather chair, his legs dangling over the side, fingering his gun. The office also had a desk and chair, and a pool table that served to divide the room. When his boys grew tired of softening up Fat Moe's already soft body, he signaled them to stop. He waited a few minutes for Moe to stop crying so he could hear what was being said to him, then got up and went to the pool table. He leaned across the green felt.

"Who the hell are you protectin', you dumb asshole? A stoolie who rats on his pals."

The second man added, "They were your pals, too. They set you up in business."

The third man said, "I guess he wants to end up like that little bitch hooker, Eve. You know what we did to her, turd?" He pointed the gun at Moe's face.

The fat man's eyes dilated in terror as the gunman squeezed the trigger. There was a terrible hiss, as though all the air had been let out of Fat Moe's balloonlike body. Moe opened his eyes to see the punching bag by his head, now deflated, swinging back and forth. The gun swung around to his temple.

"Bang-bang? They'll be able to bury you in a shoe box, Moe."

Fat Moe crumpled. In a voice that was barely a whisper, he said, "At Chun Lao's . . . the Chink's. Chinese Theater."

Two men were lifting his body off the

hook, then he was dropped to the floor like a bag of dirty laundry. Moe felt like he was going to throw up. But he was alive. In the distance he could hear the thug's voice. "You stay here with this barrel of shit."

Then there was a clanking sound and Fat Moe knew they were on the freight elevator, going down to the ground floor. He fainted before he could think about what was going to happen to Noodles.

Chun Lao's was more than a theater. In fact, as everyone knew, the theater was only a front, a cover for what went on upstairs. There were not enough customers for shadow puppet plays in all the world to pay the staff at Chun Lao's, most of whom were his relatives. He had a large family, and they all had to be fed. Chun Lao realized that everyone, especially the police, knew the theater was a front, but it didn't worry him; he paid his protection money. Paid it every week.

The shadow puppet theater was old and reeked of urine. The seats were torn, their upholstery stained and sticky. A huge Buddha, its paint chipped, sat in the rear, as though overseeing the performance and the spectators, unblinking, ancient, fully aware of all mankind's frailties. The statue, too, must have known what was beyond and above the stage, for the statue of Buddha had a nose as well as eyes. Despite the pervasive smell of urine, there was everywhere a faintly sweet odor that from time to time drifted down the back stairs. A knowledgeable person, such as an officer of the law, would recognize the smell at once. It was the smell of opium; and of death.

The stairway in the back of the theater led to a landing, beyond which were several closed doors. At the foot of the stairs sat a Chinese woman, aged, tiny, hardly larger than a rag doll. She sat erect, yet she seemed indolent, indifferent to the happiness in the theater or in the rooms above her. Only her eyes, glinting in the half-light as they made occasional sweeps of her domain, belied her indifference.

From behind her there came a slight sound and she turned to look up the stairs in time to see a man, his greasy pigtail swaying gently as he walked, carrying a tray on which rested cups and a pot of tea. He stopped and looked down at her, his eyes questioning hers. The small Chinese woman glanced toward the theater, and then imperceptibly nodded. His hand reached out and pressed on a panel between the doors. It slid open noiselessly and he slipped inside. At once the panel closed behind him, and the woman, satisfied that no security had been breached, resumed her semisomnolent position.

Inside the smoky, low-ceilinged room, fitfully lighted by old-fashioned gas jets, the Chinaman moved easily with his tray between shabby mattresses, cushions, swaybacked cots, and hemp mats. Almost every place was taken. The occupants seemed to have been there forever, their relaxed forms molded into the furnishings. Some were asleep; a few puffed on long bamboo pipes, holding the fumes deep in their lungs; others stared into space as visions danced in their warped brains, addled by the fruit of the poppy plant.

Old men and young—some in rags, others tuxedoed and manicured—lay stretched out in the room. All were equal in their abject slavery. A few women were there, too—mostly old crones, bejeweled, painted, trying to recapture a past that never existed. One young girl was among them, her youth ravaged and ruined, the bloom already faded, her hair a matted mess, unbrushed for days. All sought the same thing, none found it for more than a moment or two: bliss.

A woman moved among the sprawled bodies, padding silently, as solicitous as a nurse. She nurtured dying flames in lamps used to heat the opium, emptied the gray ashes from the pipes gone dead, refilled others. It bothered her not at all that no one was aware of her presence. She came to a man, a young man whose pipe had slipped from his grasp. Carefully she knelt down and lifted it toward his mouth. A hand touched her shoulder and she looked up. The Chinaman who had just entered the room carrying the tray motioned her away, then took her place, kneeling beside the young man.

"Noodles," he whispered. "Noodles . . ."

The young man was in no condition to answer, although he heard as from a distance his name being called. For now, it didn't matter what his dazed brain told him, he only wanted surcease, relief from the pain . . . and the pipe the girl had restored to his grasp would give him what he wanted. He took a long drag, inhaling the smoke slowly, letting it fill his lungs. His glazed eyes stared upward. There was something in his other hand, something he could feel. Slowly he moved it in front of his face and saw that it was a piece of paper, newspaper, words, harsh headlines boldly printed. . . . He knew the words, knew them now by heart, even though his eyes couldn't focus . . . didn't want to focus. Sounds, too, there were sounds he didn't want to hear—a telephone ringing, car wheels screeching, gunshots, screams, the dull thud of bodies hitting the ground . . . the telephone, he had to stop the ringing before it was too late.

Startled, he sat up in terror, reaching out, only to grasp the silk robe of the attendant, who patted him the way a father pats a baby, then eased him back onto the cot. The telephone again. He could hear it ringing, and when the ringing stopped, he would be damned to hell forever. . . .

Noodles stared at the burning wick; the flame seemed to lick diabolically near his face and he could feel the heat. Finally the telephone stopped ringing. But his dream wouldn't end. . . .

Streetlights, shimmering asphalt, it was raining . . . or had been raining. The streets were wet, slick, shining. It was cold, barely daylight, a winter's day, only yesterday, yet so long ago. He could see it, hear the sounds, yet he wasn't a part of it, just a curious onlooker, one of the crowd of morbid gapers. Only he wasn't like them, because . . .

Umbrellas. Black umbrellas, like at a funeral. He hadn't wanted to look, didn't dare to look, yet finally, in the end, he had looked, had made himself look. Death—he'd seen death before, but this was different, this time he could taste it and smell it as well as see it. And the taste was sour in his mouth, an acid bile that burned his throat, made him want to retch. That was why he needed the pipe, because of the sickness he felt. The pipe stopped that feeling, stopped the pain. The smoke burned his throat, then went to his lungs, and he relaxed. But still the pictures wouldn't go away. . . .

Acrid smoke, the skeleton of a scorched truck turned on its side, lying like a beached whale in the middle of the street, its body riddled with bullet holes. Cars everywhere, a fire truck, police running around, cursing; and then his eyes found what they sought, the bodies he didn't want to see. . . .

One of them had been driving, and his charred form, partially hanging out the door, still clung to the steering wheel. A few feet away, lying among shattered crates and broken bottles, were two more, the face of the one blown completely away. The police were busy wiring tags to the ankle of each body, stepping carefully to avoid the puddles, puddles not of water but of blood.

Noodles didn't need to get closer, didn't need to read the tags; he knew what they would say, yet he edged forward, elbowing through the throng of wide-eyed citizens, awed into silence by the finality of what they saw.

Without looking Noodles knew what was

printed on each tag. Still, he edged closer so that he could read the lettering.

PATRICK GOLDBERG, that was Patsy. And PHILLIP STEIN was Cockeye. How many years had it been since he'd thought of Cockeye's real name? And finally, although the face looked like nothing more than raw hamburger, there was MAXIMILIAN BERCOVICZ, Max, his best friend, his partner. There were tears in his eyes, he realized, and he turned away from the ravaged bodies, sickened by what he had seen, oblivious to the stares of the onlookers. There was the sound of a siren as white sheets were pulled unceremoniously over the dead bodies. No, it wasn't a siren; it was the telephone, the telephone that wouldn't stop ringing in his ears. . . .

He could see a coffin.

It was small and black and it sat in the middle of a table. Someone—no, some*thing*— was buried in it. An era was dead, a time that had made him rich. Prohibition. They were celebrating the death of Prohibition. Stupid. It had made them *all* rich.

But the coffin wasn't really a coffin; it was a chocolate cake made in the shape of a coffin, decorated with a spun-sugar ribbon. Written on the ribbon was one word: PROHI-BITION.

Fat Moe was officiating at the cake, dressed

as a chef, cutting off slices and passing them out to the milling customers. Around the cake were four magnums of champagne with lighted candles affixed to their corks. Waiters, carrying long machetelike carving knives, were busily slicing off the tops of the bottles, sending the candles toppling as the champagne bubbled forth, its froth spilling down onto the table and the coffin cake.

The room was crowded with men in tuxedos, women in evening gowns, their hands dripping with diamonds. There was an air of prosperity about the place, of success and well-being. It was a happy party, a celebration where nearly everyone was drunk. Even the more or less sober ones were laughing and screaming with delight. Everyone but Noodles, who sat at the round bar in the center of the room, grim-faced, his mind on something that was the very opposite of the general hilarity and forced gaiety going on around him.

His girlfriend, Eve, sat with him, watching him with concern. The music from the band of black musicians was all jazz, and despite her worry for Noodles, Eve couldn't help but keep time with her foot. She wanted her lover to dance with her, put his arms around her, hold her tight, and tell her what was bothering him. She spoke to him, quietly suggested that they dance, but he didn't answer her; he just solemnly shook his head in the negative and continued to stare across the room.

Her eyes followed his gaze. She saw what he saw, and she couldn't understand why it seemed so important to him. Why was he staring at Patsy and Cockeye, two of his oldest friends, with such intensity? Nothing seemed different about either of them. As usual, they were laughing uproariously at nothing at all. Her eyes flickered back toward Noodles, and she saw his gaze shift a little to the left, where Max sat next to a clinging Carol. Silently Max raised a glass in his free hand, toasting Noodles and Eve. Noodles returned the gesture, and both men drank, Max swallowing all the champagne in his glass while Noodles barely moistened his lips.

Eve said something to Noodles, but it was clear that he wasn't listening. It was as though he were hearing something from afar. She reached out to him, but he was already stumbling from the stool, pushing her aside as if he had made up his mind about something.

He had. He had to get to the telephone, to stop the ringing or . . .

Max was looking at him, trying to catch

his eye, but Noodles was already striding across the room toward the office in the back, ignoring not only Max but Cockeye as well, who was surrounded by four barely clothed young women.

Noodles bumped into Patsy, dancing with Peggy, now very fat, another old, old friend who would hate . . .

He entered the office and slammed the door behind him, shutting out the noise of the party and the accusing eyes of his friends. He looked at the telephone. Why was it ringing? He hadn't dialed yet, but he could hear the sound. His hands seemed to act on their own as he lifted the receiver from the hook and began to dial. He could hear the ringing now, logical, at the other end, ringing in the police station. His hand trembled. He had to stop before it was too late, to run away from what he was going to do, stop himself because he could see their bodies, and the opium didn't help. . . .

"Sergeant Halloran—two-three precinct. State your business."

Everything stopped as Noodles awakened from the dream to find the pipe in his hand, the old man beside him, the Chink, who was trying to tell him something.

Only the old man wasn't saying what he

wanted to hear, that it was only a dream and there was nothing to fear.

Because it wasn't a dream, and his body and brain, both now awake, knew nothing *but* fear.

CHAPTER
2

Below, on the street, the two hoods pushed through a side door of the puppet theater. They moved fast, knowing where their quarry was holed up, anxious to get him before he could escape. They wanted to end what they had started earlier in the evening, to get their job over with and to satisfy themselves that the old order of things could not be violated with impunity.

Once inside, they gave the audience the once-over and then looked past the shadow puppets toward the rear of the building where the old Chinese lady sat. The viewers didn't even notice the entrance of the two men, but the old lady, whose eyes missed nothing, caught sight of them at once. She leaned back, pretending to doze, watching them in the flickering light as they moved in her direction. She knew who they were, knew they meant trouble, but she waited. They had to come through the audience to get to her, and somewhere during that journey, when they would be out of her sight (and she would be out of theirs), she would make her move, hurry up the stairs, and sound the warning.

The killers started to slide across the back row of seats. They came to a couple locked in a fierce embrace, their faces hidden by their position of passion. Roughly, one of the hoods pulled them apart while the other flicked a cigarette lighter exposing in the dancing light a fortyish woman in faded finery and too much makeup, and a sorry-looking boy of perhaps twenty, in ragged, dirty clothes. Mandy grunted and doused the light, and the two men pushed on.

The boy, foolishly, grabbed for the heavyset man's arm, as if such meaningless heroics might impress the woman paying him for his embraces and what he would be required to do later on. The man shook him off and, when he persisted, drew a pistol from under his coat, which he calmly pointed at the boy's face. Terrified, all semblance of bravado gone, the boy released his tentative grasp and shrank back into the protective arms of the blowsy woman. Both of the hoods went on through to the aisle and started toward the back of the theater. The Chinese woman was now nowhere in sight, and although they didn't know it yet, they were too late.

There was a back stairway from the room upstairs, a fire escape that led down to the street. While the heavyset man was threatening the young man, below, the narrow door that gave out onto these steps was flung open from within. The old Chinese couple held Noodles erect, resting his armpits on their thin shoulders, as they half-carried, half-dragged him to the stairway, the man whispering encouragement to their semiconscious charge.

"Hurry, Noodles, out this way. You'll have to get yourself down the stairs. You must hurry, they'll be here in a minute. Down there, go down Mott Street and slip into Pell. In the alley. You can hide there. Hurry!"

He shoved Noodles outside and hurriedly closed the door behind him, drawing a curtain across to hide the door. Then he went to a table and picked up a teacup. The woman, he noticed, smiling to himself, had already disappeared.

They'd done what they could for him, settled the debt they owed him for arranging the protection rates for their benefactor, Chun Lao. Now they were quits and Noodles was on his own. In the street he'd be safe. Or he wouldn't. It was no concern of theirs. The debt had been paid. Honor was preserved. When he was told, Chun Lao would be pleased. If he didn't already know.

Noodles felt the air hit his face. Blinking, he shook his head. The telephone ringing had stopped. Now there were only noises, faint street noises, coming from somewhere below him. He looked at the metal steps, at the darkness below, black as a pit, blacker than his soul. Gripping the rail, slowly putting one foot forward, then the other, testing the steps as a nervous swimmer first tests the cold ocean, he started down. But before he got to the bottom, his eyes clouded over, he lost his footing and he fell, almost noiselessly, down the last few steps.

He lay there for a few minutes, waiting—until he could see again, until his breath returned, until his heart stopped beating so hard that the sound drowned out sounds of the street—then laboriously he hauled himself to his feet. His head was clear now. Clear enough for him to know that he was probably going to die. He had one chance in a million. One chance. If he could get to Fat Moe's, get the key, get the money, get away. . . .

IN MOURNING.

Those were the first words Noodles saw as he rounded the corner. He was fully awake now and much steadier than he had been. His mind was active, alert, ready for any emergency. But still the words made him stop. Yes, of course they were in mourning, all of them, Fat Moe more than any of the others except, perhaps, himself—Prohibition was over. The blinds were drawn behind the hand-lettered sign in the window of the delicatessen from his youth that had become a speakeasy as well as office and meeting place for the mob. So many things, so many years. Fat Moe's (formerly Gelly's) had been almost like home to them. No, better than home.

The air was raw with more than a hint of snow. He was glad of it, though, for the snap had held to bring him to, helped to force him to think of survival. All around him were reminders of the revelry of the night before. Signs and banners wishing good riddance to the Volstead Act; broken bottles, whole ones, too, confetti, streamers, puddles of vomit, all attested to the wild celebration. There were corpses, too. Not the kind from his nightmare that was no dream, but drunks, sleeping it off after too much cheap whiskey.

Noodles considered the front door of Moe's, then changed his mind and walked a few paces to an alley that ran along the side of the building. Peering into the gloom, he checked behind him and to his left and right until he was satisfied that no one was watching. He edged along the wall, took a key from his pocket, and inserted it in the lock. Again he paused, once more changing his mind. Leaving the key in the lock, he went farther into the darkness until he came to the outside stairs of a building that abutted Fat Moe's. Beneath them was a door. Noodles opened it and darted through.

Inside the doorway was a tiny lobby and the iron grillwork of a freight elevator. The elevator was not in sight. Noodles looked up the shaft and saw it a few floors above. He pressed the button, listened for the creak to indicate the motor had started and the elevator was on its way down, then he left the way he had come and raced back down the alley to the door where he had left the key. Silently he opened the door and went inside and moved noiselessly up the stairs.

The clank of the freight elevator woke up the triggerman guarding Fat Moe. Moe, now a heap of bloody flab, lay on the floor a few feet from the gunman. He had tried to move once or twice, but the pain proved to be too great and he had sunk back into a heap where he had been so unceremoniously dumped after the merciless beating.

Moe's guard took out his pistol, reached down, and grasped Moe by the collar, pointing the gun into his face, as he dragged the battered body across the floor toward the elevator gate. The man motioned to Fat Moe with the gun, making it clear that if Moe even briefly considered calling out a warning he was dead. Moe nodded.

The two of them stared intently at the space at the top of the gate. They could hear the elevator moving downward toward them, its clanking blotting out not only their own breathing but also the sound from across the room where a rack of billiard cues silently turned, revealing a secret passageway to the next room. The opening was black, but only for a moment, and then a figure filled its frame.

The elevator stopped. Both Fat Moe and

the gunman relaxed, for the elevator had stopped at the floor above theirs. False alarm. The hood lowered his gun. Suddenly there was a flash of light, and a hole appeared in the man's head. The hole was black for the briefest of moments, then blood gushed from it as the thug sank to the floor.

Fat Moe screamed and twisted his head, looking back across the room as Noodles, gun in hand, walked from the secret passageway into the room.

"Noodles!"

Still silent, Noodles pocketed his gun.

Fat Moe stared at him, wide-eyed, "You're alive."

"I'm alive—barely. What happened?"

Fat Moe squirmed and held up his wrists. "Untie me," he whined.

"I don't think so." He pointed toward the dead gunman. "You'd better stay like you are. You want them to think you did it? They worked you over a little, huh?"

"God, Noodles, it was awful. I—I didn't mean to tell them, but they were gonna kill me."

"It's okay, Moe. I gotta get going. Don't have much time. You understand."

"Yeah, sure. The clock."

"That's right." Noodles walked across the room to a big clock that stood against the wall. He opened the glass door and reached in, feeling for the winding key. Attached to it, tied with a piece of string, was another key. He closed the glass door and walked across the room, stepping over Fat Moe and the dead hood. Pocketing the keys, he started to leave.

"Where you going?" Fat Moe called out apprehensively.

"I don't know. To get Eve, I guess and then—"

"No! They . . . they said they already been there. And she's . . . you know."

His face a blank, Noodles turned around. "Yeah. I should have guessed. They'd go after her first." Noodles pushed the button for the elevator.

"Do you need anything, Noodles? Money?"

Holding up the two keys, Noodles laughed. It was a mirthless laugh, a deathbed laugh. "Now I got more than I need. More than I'll ever need."

"Yeah," Fat Moe said, "it's all yours now. Will I ever see you around?"

"Maybe in a few years. Maybe never. I'm gonna have to keep moving."

The elevator stopped. Noodles lifted the gate and stepped in, pulling the bars down in front of him.

As the elevator started down, Fat Moe

called out plaintively, "Why'd you do it, Noodles?"

Long after Noodles was out of sight, Fat Moe thought he heard a voice calling up from the shaft, "Do what?"

The train station was empty except for a few derelicts sleeping on the long, hard wooden benches. A ticket clerk dozed in his cage. The information booth was empty. Noodles' footsteps echoed across the marble floor. He went into a narrow alcove and approached a line of lockers. Inserting the key that he had taken from the clock case, he opened the metal door and took out a battered straw suitcase. He started to walk away, but then halted, flipped the catch, and pushed the lid open a few inches. His face filled with alarm as he stared at the contents: crumpled newspapers and old rags. His hand rummaged through the debris, hoping that underneath it there would be . . . He stopped. There was no point. He'd been taken. They all had. All those years, gone. And now he'd never know who . . . Yet of course he knew. It could have been only one person, one of them brazen enough and crazy . . . He moved away from the lockers again, slowly this time. Spotting a trash can, he dropped the suitcase and its useless contents into it. Then, squaring his shoulders, he hurried out of the station.

The station stood empty and slightly forlorn. It was the witching hour, just before dawn. Empty Pullmans and coaches, windows still dirty from their latest completed run, filled more than half the tracks and platforms. Only one train showed any sign of life. It didn't matter where it was going; it was leaving in a matter of minutes, and Noodles, as desolate and forlorn as the deserted station, had a ticket. His face was red, puffy, and unshaven; his clothes were rumpled. He wore a cheap raincoat pulled tightly around his body, its collar turned up to protect him from the damp.

A black porter, white-coated, ancient, stood nearby. The conductor looked up and down the platform. Noodles waited until the last minute, until the porter climbed aboard and the conductor moved back, then he stepped up through the door onto the train. The train began to move. Noodles waited for a moment, then walked warily into the dimly lighted car as the conductor closed the door. Noodles didn't bother to look back.

CHAPTER
3

1968

It could have been the same railroad coach, the same dust even. There was no way of telling. It definitely was the same station and possibly the same track. Over a quarter of a century had brought about a lot of changes, he supposed, but it was surprising how many things remained the same. He'd noticed that on his long trip across the country, staring out the windows at pristine farmland and grimy, run-down cities. Nothing was all that different. A lot older, but not much changed.

The country, like himself, had seen better days. The coach that had carried him on his journey was past its prime; so was he. The exterior was rough, chipped, and dented; so was his. Everything seemed a little rumpled, a little tired.

He had expected it all to be different. So far he was disappointed. New York, he told himself, must have changed. He'd seen pictures, in magazines, on TV. Big buildings, glass and granite cages. He wondered if the old neighborhood would be gone, too, torn up to be replaced by something lavish, expensive—unreal.

He thought, Everything will have been forgotten, ancient history; even those who might remember will have put it behind them. All but one. Why are you coming back? he asked himself. Good question. He remembered, when he was a child, the old rabbi who taught the Talmud. "There are only questions, David. No answers, only questions."

It was funny, the older he got, the easier it was to remember long ago. It had been a scary time. Especially at the end. It was all history, though, and he was coming back. No, he *was* back. Standing inside the station.

He looked around. It was still cavernous. More people now than when he had left.

Brighter, he thought. Ticket counters a little different. Information booth changed. Still the same old wooden benches, though, still the same smell. Loiterers, bums, perverts, cops. The usual.

Outside, it was noisy. The cabs looked different. The buses were new. But other than that, so long as he didn't look up, it seemed to be just the way he remembered it. He took a deep breath. The air tasted good. He was home.

He hailed a cab and once more asked himself, as he climbed in, why he had come back. What was the point? To find some answers, he answered himself. No, not just some answers. *The* answer. He laughed. What was the answer? A good question. Only questions. It seemed logical, then, thinking of the old rabbi, that his first stop would be the synagogue.

A giant crane caught his eye. It was lifting a granite tombstone, cradling it as gently as a baby as it set it down in the bed of a waiting truck. The cemetery by the synagogue was being torn up to make way for a new high-rise. His old neighborhood—shabby shops, drab tenements, garbage on the street, kids loitering, old people dragging along from stoop to stoop—all wiped out in the name of progress.

More memories, he thought. That's all I have now, memories of the good old days. The sign that I'm getting old, a has-been. Nowhere.

He reached into his breast pocket, checking once more to make sure the letter was there. Proof that someone remembered. Someone knew, had known all these years where he could be found. So he'd come east. Because he'd had to come. There was no use pretending he was still in hiding, because someone had sent him the letter. He was no safer there than he would be here. And at least here maybe he'd find out what had really happened. It would make him sleep easier. Make death easier. He told himself that at least now he was no longer afraid. That was something.

He looked down the street, glanced again at the cemetery, and finally turned toward the synagogue. He hoped the walls wouldn't collapse in celebration of his entry. He hadn't been inside this or any temple since he was bar-mitzvahed, more years ago than he cared to count.

A young man stepped outside into the sunlight, almost bumping into Noodles, who reached out and touched his arm.

"Excuse me, are you the rabbi? I got this letter . . . some time ago . . . about the cemetery." He held out a piece of paper, which the man in black took in his long, graceful hand.

"May I?" Noodles nodded and the man opened the letter, glancing over it quickly. "The notice we sent about the reinterment." He lowered his voice as if suddenly remembering that the mention of death might be disturbing. "Come with me."

Noodles followed him through a side door into a small, messy room that was full of filing cabinets. On one wall was a poster advertising the possibilities of beginning life anew in a country where an orange tree stood out against a cobalt-blue sky: Israel.

The rabbi, now that the light was better, looked again at the letter, reading it carefully. Finally he looked up.

"Unfortunately, you're a little late. There was a time limit. It says so right here in the second paragraph. The time limit is up, quite some time ago. Unclaimed caskets were shipped to the Bronx. When did you receive this letter?"

"About a week, ten days ago. I drove here as soon—"

"That's impossible. We sent them out six

or seven months ago. See the date. There was plenty of time. . . . Let me check, just to make sure. Just the underlined names?"

"Yes. Just those three."

The rabbi turned to one of the metal cabinets, opened a drawer, and pulled out several files, flipping through them. Under his breath, as if to himself, he said, "Maximilian Bercovicz . . . yes. Patrick Goldberg . . . yes. And"—he glanced at the letter—"yes .. Philip Stein . . . No, that's a surprise. They didn't go to . . . they were reclaimed and all three have been reinterred in Riverdale."

Noodles looked at him blankly, and the young man, misinterpreting, added, "A beautiful place. It's like a big garden. Clean, with fresh air. A nice place to live, too." He frowned at his own levity. "Are you a relative?"

"No."

The rabbi squinted. "Strange. These letters were sent only to relatives, those we could find, who were still alive and in the neighborhood or who had left a forwarding address. Your name is . . . ?"

Looking straight at him, Noodles replied, "Williams. Robert Williams."

He held up the envelope. It was addressed

to Robert Williams. The rabbi looked bewildered. "Williams isn't usually a Jewish name." He picked up the register on top of the cabinet and leafed to the Ws. "Just as I thought. We didn't send you any letter."

The purple neon sign outside reflected through the window. The sign had seen better days; the neon was flickering and several of the letters were out completely. Above the sign was the owner's name. For the few old-timers left it meant continuity; for them it suggested that the cuisine might at least be Jewish if not kosher. The newer residents of the area did not particularly care.

FAT MOE'S had seen many changes, and not only in name. Time had taken its toll. It had originally been a deli, run by Moe's father. Then it had been a speakeasy. Now it was a sort of deli once again, one that sold booze along with salami, pastrami, and sour pickles. Moe had tried to modernize the place, but his attempts had not been completely successful. Profits had fallen off when the ethnic makeup of the neighborhood shifted, so the job had been abandoned. Still, the place was clean.

Time had taken its toll on Moe as well. He was still heavy, but now his hair was thin and gray. He tried to keep himself and the place up, but he was always a little tired—and his feet never stopped aching. On top of everything else, his teeth were going.

There were a few customers in the place, finishing their beers before going home for the night. They all looked up when the phone rang. Moe walked to the wall where it hung, slightly irritated by its insistent ring. Who could be calling at this time of night? A wrong number, that was who. These days he got more wrong numbers than any other kind of call. He was tempted not to answer, but was afraid the ringing wouldn't stop. He let his curiosity get the best of him. Maybe, he thought, I've been left a fortune by some unknown relative in the old country.

He had hardly got the receiver in his hand when the voice on the other end began to speak. His face turned ashen and his jaw dropped. Lowering his voice, he answered, at the same time wiping the sweat from his face on the sleeve of his shirt. Then he put the phone down without hanging up and went back to the customers, urging them to leave. When the last one had gone, he slumped into a chair.

From that vantage point he could see out the window. His hand still held the receiver and he slowly reached up and returned it to its hook. Shaking with terror, he forced himself to stand up. He went to the wall, turned off the inside lights, and pulled down the shades. He started toward the side door that opened onto the alley, the one now used for deliveries, but he was not halfway across the room when the piercing sound of the doorbell ripped through the room. Noodles, he now knew, had been watching. But for how long? A minute, an hour, a day? Longer, even?

Numbly he went to the side door, and making sure the security chain was on, he opened it as far as the chain would allow. He peeked out and the face he saw—older, wrinkled, weathered, a face that had been burned into his memory—peered back at him.

"I brought back the key to your clock." The old password. It was Noodles, all right, not some kind of trick. Opening the door, Moe wasn't sure if that was better or worse.

Noodles, carrying a suitcase, slipped by him. Looking around, he made sure the place was empty, before reaching into his pocket to remove the two keys.

Frightened as he was, Fat Moe was excited by Noodles' return. Moe hurried after him, moving around so that he could see his face in the light from the bar, and reached out to embrace him. "Noodles . . . God you're a sight for sore eyes. I thought sure you'd bought it, one way or the other."

"Lock the door. So I don't buy it for a little while longer."

"Sure, Noodles, sure. Anything you say."

While Fat Moe was noisily locking and chaining the door, Noodles looked around. The room was the same, yet it was different, too. The bar was where the kitchen had been, and there was a moth-eaten pool table, perhaps the same one from the old days. The few tables were sticky with damp circles where beer bottles and glasses had stood; the walls and ceiling were slightly stained from leaking pipes. Fat Moe, he decided, had not prospered in the years since they had said their good-byes.

From across the room, Fat Moe turned and asked, "When d'ya get back?"

"Today."

"Where you been?" When Noodles didn't answer, Moe continued, "Why? Why d'ya come back, Noodles?"

"They got in touch with me."

"Who? Who got in touch with you?"

Noodles leaned against the bar. "Don't you know?"

"Me? That's a laugh. I don't know nothin' 'bout nobody no more. I can't even get a book or the numbers. I'm out in the cold. It's all different now. Me, I got no contacts. No one from the old days is even alive. Except you. And I thought you was gone, Noodles. I thought either they found you or you just up and died from somethin' or other."

"Yeah, I really didn't think it could have been you. You gonna offer me a drink?"

"You bet. On the house, the best we got." Moe scurried behind the bar, picked up a glass, eyed it critically, wiped it with his apron, eyed it again, and satisfied, put it on the bar. Then he grabbed a bottle and started to fill the glass. As he poured, Noodles reached into his pocket and took out an envelope, which he slid along the counter to Fat Moe. Moe pushed the glass to him and picked up the envelope while Noodles sat at a table.

"Who's Robert Williams?" Moe asked.

"I am."

Following the lines with his finger, Moe started to read the letter aloud. " 'We wish to inform you that as a result of the sale of Beth Israel cemetery in . . .' Hey, I got one of these on account of my father, *alav-ha-sholom,* may he rest in peace. Who you got buried there?" Before he could read any further, Noodles got up and took the envelope from him.

"Mine didn't come from the synagogue."

"It didn't? Who, then?"

"And there's a little p.s. with mine: 'Dear Noodles. Even though you're hiding in the asshole of the world, we found you.' It also says, 'We haven't forgotten you. Get ready.' "

"For what?"

"That it doesn't say."

"The names in there, did you underline them? You know, the three . . . ?"

"It came like that. Just like that. Underlined." Noodles folded the letter and stuck it back in the envelope.

"What d'ya think it means, Noodles? What d'ya think?"

"I think . . . I think the answer's here. That's why I came back. To find the answer."

They stood staring at each other, the silence broken only by the ticking of the clock. Fat Moe looked at it, walked across the room, and wound it some more. "Still works. What do you think of that? Sounds better than *my* ticker."

Not bothering to answer, Noodles drained his glass before he asked, "Got a bed for me?"

Moe shrugged. "Nobody here but Fat Moe." He picked up the suitcase Noodles had brought. "Come on."

Taking in the room, Noodles started to follow Fat Moe. "You know," he said, "I always wondered if you had helped yourself to that million dollars. Now I know. You're on your ass worse than ever."

Fat Moe was through the door already and turning on a light in the passageway.

"But I thought . . . you got it all."

"You thought wrong. The suitcase was empty."

They were in the room that had served as the office for the mob. Nothing was left of the old days.

Fat Moe dropped the bag. "Then who took it?"

"That's what I've been asking myself for over thirty years."

Sensing that Noodles was thinking of how the room used to look, Moe said, "I moved everything that was left in here. Like storage. I had to sell the house and the back room. I just got the bar and this left. And my room. If it bothers you here, you can have my room. I can sleep here. I don't mind."

"This'll be fine. Thanks anyway."

Noodles wandered around the room while Fat Moe took out sheets and a pillow from the desk drawer. Finding what he had been looking for—a photograph—Noodles stopped and examined the faded snapshot of a pretty young girl in a ballet costume, up on her toes, her arms curling upward like the wings of a dragonfly.

"And your sister?" Noodles asked, keeping his voice even.

"Ain't seen her for years now. She doesn't remember I exist. She's a big star, you know?" He started making up a bed on the couch.

"I knew. Funny thing is, we all should have known right from the beginning. You can pick winners at the starting gate—the winners and the losers. Who woulda bet a penny on you?"

"No one. I was always a loser. But Deborah ... and you, Noodles. I'd a put everything I had on you.

"Yeah, well, you woulda lost, Moe."

Moe shrugged, flashed an awkward smile, showing his dentures. "Your bed's made up. You look beat, huh?"

"Right. I'm beat."

"Okay. 'Night."

" 'Night." Noodles wearily lifted his suitcase and put it on the table. As he flipped the lock, he sensed that Fat Moe was still in the room. He paused, but didn't look up.

Finally Moe said, "Noodles ... ?"

"Yeah?

"What you been doin' all these years?"

Very slowly Noodles replied, "Going to bed early."

When Fat Moe was gone, Noodles turned back to the table with the photographs. There were a lot of pictures of himself, sometimes alone, sometimes with three other men about the same age, all grinning, happy, cocky. There was one at the beach, one in an open touring car, one at the races, another at the dog track. Always smiling, always sure. The four of them had the world by the balls. Of course, it hadn't begun that way. In the beginning they had all been like Fat Moe, destined to be losers. . . .

A song came back to him, one he hadn't heard in years. "Amapola," it was called. "My pretty little poppy . . ." He picked up the picture of the girl, then quickly put it down and left the room, walking back into the darkened bar that had once been a lunchroom.

The bittersweet strains of the music beckoned him as he turned on a light and went behind the bar for a bottle and a glass. The sound seemed to be coming from the direction of the narrow door at the far end of the room. Holding the bottle and glass, he walked toward it as if in a trance. The music grew louder.

He knew what would be behind the door even before he opened it. Some things never changed. Plumbing, for instance. An ordinary little john with a toilet, urinal, a washbasin, and near the ceiling a rectangular air vent with a grating over it.

He rested the bottle and glass down on the sink and climbed up onto the seat of the john. From there, standing on tiptoe, he could see through the vent into the next room. The music grew louder. Sunlight seemed to filter through the vent. Beyond, the victrola was playing and she was dancing while a ragged boy watched her wide-eyed. . . .

CHAPTER

4

1925

"Amapola, my pretty little poppy."

Sunlight flooded the room as the young
girl danced about, in leotard and ballet
slippers. Slim and still boyish in build, she
was about thirteen, but there was, despite
the sweetness of her smile, a look about the
eyes that suggested she knew more than her
years should have allowed.

There was clutter in the room—brooms
and mops and buckets as well as trunks and
crates and boxes of empty bottles—yet the
girl danced among them as though she were

in a field of the flowers in her song. On the walls hung posters advertising Lucky Strikes, Moxie, and Coca-Cola, lively, colorful, and vibrant, but none as vibrant as the girl.

A windup victrola, the kind with a horn, was perched on a crate, spinning its revolutions, sending the music beyond the room. "Amapola, my pretty little poppy . . ."

The girl danced with an angular grace, the movements, like her figure, still slightly raw and unformed. But she danced with power and concentration and the carefree abandon of someone who knows her own talent and also knows that she is not unadmired, who in fact knows at that very moment she is being watched through the grating in a corner of the room near the ceiling.

She knew her audience well, and the knowledge of who it was gave her pleasure as well as an intoxicating sense of power. Despite this, her brow was furrowed in concentration, and the pleasure she felt would not have been apparent to an onlooker; in fact, it was not apparent to the fourteen-year-old voyeur with dirty, mussed hair wearing patched, seedy clothes.

David Aaronson was not tall enough to see through the grate by standing, even on tiptoe, on the seat of the toilet, so he was balanced shakily on a crate that he had put on top of the seat. Each time she danced by, her head held high, he ducked down, afraid that she might see him peering through the grate. When there was no cry of outrage, he resumed his position, looking out again in a mixture of wonder, admiration, and adolescent lust.

The visions that danced through his head were rudely interrupted by the opening of the door to the room he was watching, as a fat boy of about his own age waddled in wearing a floor-length white apron. The boy was sweaty and harried as he looked back over his shoulder.

"Deborah," he called plaintively, "Papa says you should stop with the dancin' and make with the apron. We got customers all over the place waiting for lunch."

Without missing a beat in her movements and without looking at her brother, the girl replied, "No."

"I can't do everything, you know, Deborah. You and your dancing lessons. Papa's gonna get mad."

"So let him."

"He gets mad he don't hit you, it's me he comes after. That ain't fair."

The girl kept on dancing and the fat boy retreated to the door.

He turned and whined, "Honest. I can't do everything."

"Try," was his sister's answer.

Angry, he steamed out of the room, slamming the door behind him. She called after him through the closed door. "Besides, I got my elocution lesson."

Finally the record ran down, and the girl, breathing heavily, stopped her movements. Casually she glanced up at the grate and then positioned herself so that, as she bent to untie her toe shoes, her round little bottom was turned in the grate's direction. Provocatively, with her back to the boy she knew was watching her, she wiggled her narrow hips out of her leotard and placed her shoes and leotard in a bag. Then, wearing only panties, but still with only her back exposed, she picked up a dress that hung across the back of a chair, slipped it over her head, and wriggled some more until it slid down and covered her slim frame.

Finished dressing, Deborah pirouetted once around the room, her skirt flouncing, then went into the deli with its clamor of shouted orders and men arguing, making deals, boisterous and full of life. The large room was clean, tidy, and attractive. Countermen and cooks were preparing sandwiches and hot plates, soups and delicacies, while waiters with heavy-laden trays swiveled their way between the packed tables. Most of the customers—in fact, all but a few—were Jews, Ashkenazim from eastern Europe, most of them still bearded and wearing hats, but already adapted to American business clothes.

The proprietor, Gelly, was the father of the fat boy, Moe, and the young dancer, Deborah. Gelly stood in a patriarchal pose at the front door, keeping an eye on the help, the customers, and most especially, the cash register.

Deborah crossed the room, maneuvering between the throng of customers and waiters until she came to where her father was positioned.

"I'm going, Tateh," she said.

"Be careful, little one."

Her hand on the doorknob, she turned and called out to her brother, "Fats, you better spray the toilet. I saw a cockroach in there." With a sprightly flip of her head, as if bowing to an applauding audience, she ran outside.

The boy who had so joyously watched her cavorting from the john was stung by the wisecrack. In a rage, angry and humiliated, he jumped down from the crate only to bump into an unwary man who was at that moment using the urinal.

Noodles ran out as the man screamed after him a string of Yiddish curses. Noodles ignored the shouts, and plowing past the customers and nearly colliding with Moe, who was precariously balancing a tray of pastrami and corned-beef sandwiches, he pushed through the door, looking frantically up and down the street. He caught sight of Deborah, then started after her.

He had gone only a few feet when he ran into three of his friends. The streets were crowded not only with kids about their own age, but with all sorts of humanity. Hawkers with pushcarts; Hasidic Jews in their long black coats and bearded faces that no razor had ever touched; women dressed as in the old country, in long skirts and shawls, sometimes with a babushka around the throat, sometimes around the head; men in rags, begging; sleekly dressed, olive-skinned Arabs steering potential customers toward one or another of the street's many stores; wide-eyed children, hunger etched on their already-lined faces; an occasional Chinese, hurrying toward his job at the laundry ironing shirts; European Jews in suits and ties, busy merchants aspiring to become captains of industry; red-faced policemen dressed in blue, their heavy billy clubs tapping time on their legs as they walked—all part of the glorious American experiment called the melting pot, trying to hustle a buck, feed a family, build a life and a future, all, like Noodles and his teen-aged gang, looking for a way out . . . and up.

Actually only two of them, Patsy and Cockeye, were the same age as Noodles; the third, Dominic, was several years younger—small, skinny, and feral. They all wore the same uniform, the uniform of the Lower East Side streets: ratty, patched, cast-off clothes, either too large or too small; worn down, scuffed shoes; and peaked caps.

There was excitement in the air as the three caught up with Noodles; they were keyed-up, nervous, and jumpy.

"Noodles," Patsy called out, "wait up."

"Bugsy wants to see us. He's got a job." It was Dominic, smaller than the others, who whispered this illicit information.

"Later," was Noodles' only answer. "I got business." He scurried by them and started to run, dodging passersby, until he turned a corner where Deborah, hoping that he would chase after her, loitered, pretending to look in the window of a store that sold cheap dresses.

"Who you callin' a cockroach?" Noodles grabbed her long black braid, forcing her to turn around.

It hurt, his pulling that way, but her face showed no pain. She had learned a long time ago, from watching the pitiful existences of the people around her, that in strength lay her passage to a better life. "Well, what *are* you, David Aaronson? You're filthy. You make me sick. You crawl up toilet walls just like a roach. So, what are you? Answer me that. Go ahead, answer." She twisted her head and pulled free from his grasp. "Let go."

"I make you sick, so how come you showed me your tush?"

Her voice dripping with scorn, Deborah answered, "To a roach? I should care about what a roach sees?" She pointed at the store window where both of them were reflected in the sunlight. "So, look at yourself. A roach."

As his eyes left her face and found his image in the window, he saw her reflection turn and run off, skipping between pushcarts, not looking back. He stared at himself, and what he saw was depressing. She was right, he thought: a roach. Suddenly there were four images in the window, four roaches. Three of them were snickering, having observed the scene with the girl.

Trying to be a man of the world and pass off the incident, Noodles said to them, "If she don't leave me alone, I'm gonna give her what she keeps askin' for." When he detected skepticisim in the eyes of his friends, he quickly changed the subject, becoming all business. "What's Bugsy want?"

"We gotta wake up a deadbeat," Patsy told him.

"Yeah," Cockeye added, "that schmuck at the newsstand ain't paid his dues."

Monkey's was not a high-class joint, even by the low-class standards of the surrounding neighborhood. It was frequented by the least savory types of that area: small-time hoods, drifters and grifters, men with a dollar earned in a variety of dishonest ways. But, as always, there were a few customers who looked and acted as if they could pay their way, not only at Monkey's but anywhere, a few who looked as if they might be earning legitimate money. Without them, Monkey might have been hard-pressed to break even, except for the fact that he was involved to some degree in most of the rackets that took place around him. He sold illegal booze, took illegal bets, hid illegal weapons as well as illegal aliens, acted as a front, a go-between, and anything else he could do to keep on the good side of the racketeers who lived in—and controlled—the neighborhood. He also engaged in payoffs whenever it was necessary for the payer not to be seen giving money to the payee.

It was this subject—payoffs—that Monkey was discussing with Noodles, Cockeye, Patsy, and Dominic. "Do you want the dollar or the drunk?" he was asking, hoping their answer would be the latter. When they hesitated, he asked them to repeat what they had done so that he could report it verbatim to Bugsy. He hoped to buy some time, so that some drunk would get drunker and therefore look easier, a better choice than the dollar, which he could then pocket. Monkey, a middle-aged man with a paunch and a worried expression, was, as he often exclaimed, nobody's fool.

Dominic, despite being the youngest and the smallest, was the most articulate of the four, the best teller of tales. Affecting a gravelly tough-guy voice, he recounted again what the group had just pulled off.

"It was real easy, Monkey," he bragged. "Like I told you before. Anytime you need anything done, just tell Bugsy to call on us."

"So, tell me again, you little putz, how you did it. It'll help keep me warm on cold winter nights." He laughed at his own joke and the boys joined in.

"Go on, Dom," Patsy urged. "Tell Monkey how we done it."

"Well, we waited until nobody was around the newsstand and Baldy Lebowitz was half-asleep inside, and then we sneaked as close as we could; we all had matches and Noodles, he lights his first and he holds it up to a paper that's hanging on the side, and then we all done the same kind of thing all around the stand and we kept lightin' things, and there was some trash on the street and we lit that too, and before you knew it the whole damn thing was on fire. So old Baldy, all of a sudden he comes awake and he runs out and he's screaming for somebody to get him some water and everybody's standing around watching, but by the time they got the water, it was too late, the whole thing was all burned up.

"And us, we just run away—walked away, really—and watched from the corner, and then we run right over here to collect from Bugsy for doing the job right."

"Right. That's good work, all of yas! I'll tell Bugsy."

Cockeye said, "So can we have our dollar?"

"Sure, if that's what you want." Monkey looked at a drunk at the bar. When no one said anything, he hustled them along, saying, "C'mon. Make up your minds."

"Noodles, let's take the dollar," Cockeye said.

Noodles ignored him and pointed at a different drunk. "Him."

"Are you sure? You know he ain't drunk yet, kid. Not enough."

"Bugsy said," Noodles answered, "he'd give us a dollar or we could roll a drunk."

"Are you nuts? Take that other guy." Monkey was beginning to lose his patience.

Dominic pushed himself beside Noodles and said, "We'll wait."

"Roll the first guy, he's really drunk."

"What's to roll?" Noodles replied. "He's drunk it all up."

"Okay," an exasperated Monkey answered, "I want you out of here. See that one?" He pointed to a fat little man who wore a gold chain in his vest. The man was bleary-eyed and weaving. "Him—or no one."

Noodles shrugged. "So bounce the little shikker."

As the boys started out the back door to wait for their prey, Monkey called over two of his bouncers and held a whispered conversation with them. Then he went into a back room to call Bugsy while the two hulks went over to the little man wearing the vest with the watch chain, picked him up by his jacket and the seat of his pants, and carried him to the door. The man was mumbling something, but his speech was incoherent and he offered no real resistance when he was tossed out and landed unceremoniously in the gutter. Noodles watched from the back door to make sure the man had been bounced, and then he ran out to join the others, who were waiting in the alley. They were watching the drunk, who had regained his feet and was now zizzagging from lamppost to lamppost.

Tense and silent, not totally fearless, the boys followed at a distance. The drunk lurched through the tumultuous streets, oblivious not only to those around him, who gave him a wide berth, but also to the boys who were stalking him. They had spotted a dark alley ahead and whipped past him, pretending to be involved in an idle game, then ducked into the shadowy alley, an ideal spot for divesting someone of his valuables.

Once in the alley Noodles whispered to Cockeye, "Jacket," and at once Cockeye slipped out of his grubby coat and, lifting it above his head, held it ready like a net. The other three huddled in the shadows, ready to pounce. The drunk came into a view, but just behind him, on the other side of the street, was an unwelcome sight: a large, lumbering red-faced cop, strolling along his beat, occasionally nodding to shopkeepers and passersby but keeping a wary eye out not only for criminals but also, being a typical New

York policeman in almost every respect, opportunities to supplement his meager pay and enrich himself in either cash or goods. He was not a popular man in the neighborhood, for it was believed—and not without justification—that he was as bent on plunder as much of the criminal element, and that he was in cahoots with the men who ran the neighborhood rackets.

"Shit," Dominic hissed to the others. "Whitey the Fartface!"

"Shit," Noodles repeated and the other two echoed the expression yet again.

Alarmed and furious, they shrank back, hoping that he hadn't spotted them and that there would still be a way to take their quarry without drawing the attention of the burly lawman, who had stopped at the corner and was peering up and down the street as he idly swung his billy club.

The boys groaned. Whitey looked as if he were about to become a permanent fixture on the corner.

"We shoulda took the dollar," Cockeye moaned.

"We coulda had ten hot corned-beef sandwiches on poppy-seed rolls at Gelly's," Patsy, perpetually hungry, added.

"A dollar. A whole dollar," Dominic added.

"That's a quarter a piece. A whole quarter," he added.

"Look!" Noodles said, pointing down the street. A horse-drawn wagon was coming down the street from the other direction. Heaped with old battered furniture which was tied down with frayed cords and topped by a towheaded boy about their age playing king of the mountain, the cart had drawn even with the drunk. An old woman wearing a babushka sat in front, urging the ancient horse on.

"The wagon'll hide us from old Fartface. C'mon, you guys, get ready," Noodles whispered.

Whitey the cop was still in view, but the wagon had drawn almost abreast of him, and in a few more seconds it would blot him from their view—and them from his. The drunk continued to stagger along. They would have only a few seconds, but Noodles calculated that it would be enough time for them to knock him down and strip him clean of his jewelry and cash. The others crowded behind him, ready for the ambush.

They hadn't figured on the blond boy on the wagon, however, who had also spotted the drunk as well as the four would-be muggers. With one leap he swooped down from the wagon, landing at the tipsy man's feet, right between him and the four boys. Ignoring them entirely, he put his arm around the drunk like a Good Samaritan and supported the man's weight. His eyes glistened like a wolf's, but there was an angelic smile on his face as he said, "You sick, mister? Huh? You sick? You want some help, huh? C'mon, I'll help you. You want to go somewhere? You're worse than my uncle Nathan. What do you wanna get soused for anyway? It'll just get your old lady mad at you. You're so bad you can't even talk. Come on, you can ride with me."

With surprising strength for someone his size, he got the drunk under the arms and hiked him up onto the wagon, which was still moving along at its snail's pace. Then the blond, with agility that matched his strength, jumped up beside the man and put his arm possessively around his shoulders as though shielding him from a cruel world.

He grinned down at the four boys, who just stood there, mouths agape, speechless, too surprised to say anything, as the wagon moved away. Finally Noodles shook his head in disbelief and said, "C'mon, that guy's ours. Stick close to the wagon."

The boys started off, but they were halted by a bellicose voice from across the street. "Stop!"

They froze in their tracks, turned, and attempted to assume poses that were meant to be the picture of innocence.

Moving lightly on his feet for so big a man, swaggering slightly, but not hurrying, Whitey the cop crossed the street.

"What are you kids doin' here?" he demanded, his speech thick with a heavy brogue.

The boys looked at one another.

Patsy said, "What are we kids doing here?"

Noodles watched the wagon disappearing around the corner and answered with resignation, "What are we doin' here? We're gettin' it up the ass, that's what we're doin'."

"Yeah," Cockeye added, "gettin' screwed. Is there a law against it?"

Whitey spread his legs and stood staring at the boys, tapping his billie against his leg. The boys stared back, but finally were forced to look away. Cockeye reached into his pants pocket and pulled out a small tin flute, which he put to his lips, and began to blow a cheerful little march. Patsy looked at Noodles, and the two of them laughingly linked arms around each other's waists and began dancing down the street to the time of the music, Cockeye following. Dominic lingered for a moment, then took off his cap, and passing dangerously close to the cop, much like a daring bullfighter, held out the cap and asked plaintively, "Spare a dime for four poor pisherkehs?"

Whitey aimed a foot at Dominic's rear, but the boy sensed the kick was coming and increased his speed just enough to avoid the blow. He scooted on after the other three, catching up with them at the end of the block, where the four of them turned and thumbed their noses at Whitey before rounding the corner.

CHAPTER
5

It wasn't the worst building on the block, but you would not have had an easy time convincing the tenants of that. Lower East Side tenements, jammed one against the next, stretched endlessly for as far as the eye could see. And looking down the next block, you would see very much the same thing. Stores on the ground-floor level were at every corner and often in midblock, too, as tailor shops, laundries, and mom-and-pop groceries sprang up, failed, were replaced by new proprietors who tried other lines of business, failed, and then were replaced by still others. There were stoops where kids hung out, and old people, too, when the weather was decent or when it was so unbearably hot they couldn't remain inside. Leading to the stoops were flights of steep steps where makeshift games could be played, fights could begin, or when it was very dark, furtive love could be made.

Inside, one building was much like the next. Long, narrow halls, dimly lit, that smelled of cabbage (a staple of the neighborhood), urine, and beer were lined with boxes, broken-down baby carriages, wagons, and junk of all sorts—things perhaps too valuable to throw away yet, but not so valuable that it wasn't worth taking a chance on having them stolen to get a little more precious space in the tiny cramped apartments.

Space was never plentiful, nor was food. Only people were plentiful; too many of them crowded into the buildings, the apartments, the neighborhood. Rats were plentiful, too, foraging among the garbage cans and sometimes venturing up from the musty basements into the rooms and lives of the humans; vermin were plentiful; roaches were plentiful; disease was plentiful, and death, following that. Births, too, were plentiful, for in crowded spaces with no money for entertainment and frequently none for food or fuel, there was little left to do to forget the misery but seek solace in the arms of another human being.

Hope, on the other hand, was in short supply. Among the young, who noticed the poverty and degradation less, hope still flourished. Their parents and grandparents, though, beaten down by the struggle to merely survive, had long since given up hope, long ago realized that the promise of America was an empty dream. These streets were definitely not paved with gold.

For the young, who felt the pain but felt it less acutely, there was still a chance. Good fortune could come their way. A nickel might drop from a pocket in front of your very eyes, lying there on the cement waiting for you to pick it up. There might be a job running an errand, where the reward would be an apple or a piece of candy. A rich man might smile at you, if you were a girl, and young and pretty, and you would be whisked away to a life of luxury and ease.

Or . . . you could become a criminal.

Crime meant money. It meant fancy suits, felt hats, wing-tipped shoes, three-course meals featuring meat, accompanied by a stein of beer, a glass of wine, a shot of rye. It meant haircuts in barber shops, with talcum and after-shave. It meant power, respect, being feared by others rather than having to

fear them. But, most of all, for a fourteen-
year-old male, it meant an endless succes-
sion of that most mysterious of commodities,
girls.

It was not girls, however, that were on
Noodles' mind as he and Patsy, dejected
and weary, climbed the stairs of the tenement where they lived. He felt defeated for
the moment. It wasn't just the money; it
was everything. It was Whitey and the blond
kid who stole the drunk from them (Noodles
had no illusions about the kid's intentions
toward the drunk); it was Monkey, who used
them and felt contempt for them; it was
Bugsy, who ran the neighborhood (Noodles
hoped someday to work for him full-time,
but Bugsy for now thought of him as nothing
more than a punk kid). And it was what faced
him when he got home, more bad news.

"So long," he said as he turned off at his
floor.

Patsy continued on up, calling down,
"Yeah, so long." There was a pause, then
Patsy came back down a few steps to where
Noodles stood rooted. "Ain't you goin' home?"

"What for? My old man's prayin' and my
old lady's cryin', we got no lights 'cause they
turned off the electric when we didn't pay
the bill. There won't be nothin' to eat, either,
except maybe boiled beets. Home! I'm gonna

sit on the pot and read." He reached into his pocket and pulled out a dog-eared, torn book he'd found in a trash can. Holding it up, he marched down the hall to the communal john, pushed the door open, and went inside as Patsy went back up the stairs.

After he had relieved himself and flushed, Noodles stayed where he was, comfortably ensconced on the can, reading the book he had found, *Martin Eden*. He had been reading for some time when he heard footsteps coming down the hall in his direction. He bent forward and looked through the keyhole. Coming toward him was a girl about his own age, not very pretty but with round hips and heavy breasts. Silently he undid the chain and then sat back.

The girl tried the door, found it unlocked, and opened it. She stopped short when she saw him, but didn't turn away. Flashing what he thought was his most winning smile, he waved the book and said, "Hi, Peggy."

She looked down at him unfazed. "At least you could lock the door."

Noodles pointed in the direction of his crotch. His voice was shaky as he asked, "Don't you like it?"

Peggy shrugged. "What's to like? I seen better."

"Uh-huh. You seen lots, I suppose."

Coquettishly, Peggy asked, "How many girls you seen? I'll tell you how many. None. That's how many girl's privates you seen."

Afraid to deny it, knowing she'd hear the lie in his voice, Noodles said, "Hey, lemme see yours."

"Sure. Why not?" She hiked her skirts up above her panties. Involuntarily Noodles reached out, but she quickly dropped her skirt, like a curtain, letting it fall over the about-to-be-experienced unknown.

"Looksies," she said, backing away from his grasp. "No feelsies."

Noodles stood up and awkwardly grabbed her, groping for her breasts as he tried to kiss her.

Enjoying teasing him, she let him fondle her for a moment and then pulled away. "Uh-huh. None of that."

"How come? Don't you like it?"

"I like it okay. But not for free. Bring me something special to eat, from the bakery. Then I'll let you. Bring me one of them charlotte things and I'll let you do any thing you like, Noodles."

"Anything?"

"Anything. With lots of whipped cream. You know the kind I mean."

"Tomorrow. Tomorrow I'll bring you one." He grabbed for her again.

She slapped his hand and said, "I don't give no credit. And stop squeezin' me so hard or I'll poop in my pants." He dropped his hands as if he'd been struck, and she added, "Bring it tomorrow and I'll let you." When he didn't say anything, she asked, "Well, you gettin' out?" She pulled up her skirt, dropped her underpants, and sat before he could see anything.

He buttoned up his pants and disgustedly kicked the door shut behind him. Then he ran down the hall, down the stairs, and out into the fresh air. He was angry, looking for a fight, anything to relieve the tension.

Hungry and frustrated, the first thing he saw when he came down the steps from his tenement was the blond kid who'd stolen the drunk. The son of a bitch was moving in right across the street! He was busily unloading the wagon under the watchful eyes of most of the residents of the building he and his family were moving into.

The wise-ass, Noodles thought. The kid was about his own size and Noodles was pretty sure he could take him. Here was Noodles' chance to get even. Then he remembered how strong the blond had been, how easily he'd lifted the drunk and vaulted into the wagon. It didn't matter, he decided. This was his territory, the drunk had been given to them, however indirectly, by Bugsy, and Bugsy controlled the neighborhood rackets. The kid was going to have to learn that. Noodles started across the street.

The boy was unloading an old-fashioned box camera, the kind that sat on a tripod, and once he had it down from the wagon, he put the camera on its stand and bent over to look into it. It was pointed in Noodles' direction, and Noodles, when he saw the kid looking at him through the lens, deliberately turned around, bent over, and aimed his backside at the kid, slapping his rump derisively, as good a challenge as he could think of. "Gimme six copies," he called out.

The kid brought his head up and peered over the camera. "Drop your pants and I'll not only give you six, I'll stick it up yours again."

"Huh!" Noodles came across the street threateningly. "What d'ya mean, again?"

The boy could see that Noodles was out for blood, so he pretended to busy himself with organizing the things that were to be taken inside the building. "It's a long story." He reached into his pocket and provocatively brought out a gold watch attached to a chain that Noodles immediately recognized as the one that had been looped through the vest of the drunk.

The kid looked at the watch and added, "And look what time it is." He smiled a shit-eating grin. "It's already seven thirty-four and I got work to do." He held up the watch, letting it swing on the chain. "See? Or can't you tell time?" He replaced the watch in his pocket, and with the grin still on his face, he easily lifted a heavy crate that had a glass lamp balanced on top.

Noodles was impressed by the kid's strength as he followed him up the front stairs. When they came to the door, Noodles stepped in front of him and said, "Allow me." With one hand he opened the door, with the other he helped himself to the watch, taking it from the kid's pocket while he stood there, helpless, still clutching the heavy crate with the glass lamp perched precariously on top.

Noodles looked at the watch. "Now it's seven thirty-five, and I ain't got a damn thing to do. Except tell time."

Furious, but unable to do anything, the kid replied evenly, "All right, asshole. I'll do something with your time. Like maybe put you to sleep." He tottered back down the stairs and started to put the crate back on the wagon, but Noodles jumped by him and took the horse by the reins, pulling the animal forward just enough so the kid couldn't get the crate on the moving wagon.

Holding the horse and walking backward, Noodles, in his most sinister sneer, said, "Since we're talking about time, it looks to me like you're gonna break that be-yoo-tee-ful lamp at seven thirty-six." He looked at the watch again. "I give you fifteen seconds."

He took another step backward and bumped into someone. When he turned to see who was behind him, he was confronted by the broad expanse of Whitey the cop.

Before Noodles could react, Whitey had snatched the watch from him. "Were'd you pink this, you little ganef?"

"It's mine," Noodles replied with righteous indignation. "Give it back."

"Prove it, ganef. Prove it's yours."

The blond kid had finally managed to get the crate and lamp back on the wagon. Red-faced from the exertion, he rushed up to them and to Noodles' surprise, he said, "He's telling the truth, Officer. I gave it to him."

Whitey scrutinized him carefully, from broken-down shoes to smudged face. "Yeah. And who the hell are you?" He moved menacingly forward. "I ain't never seen you around here. What neighborhood you from?"

"From the Bronx. We're just movin' in."

"I see. And up in the Bronx they give away watches to strangers, huh? So you're gonna start the same practice on my beat? In a pig's ass you are."

The kid pointed to Noodles and said, "He's my uncle. No kiddin'. Go ask my mom."

Ignoring this sally, Whitey asked, "And who gave the watch to you? Don't tell me you bought it."

"My other uncle. My uncle Nathan."

Noodles chimed in. "He's my little brother. Nate, we call him. You seen him around."

"Wise-asses, both of you." The cop pointed to the blond kid and said, "You tell your uncle Nathan to stop by the precinct." He flipped the watch in the air by the chain, catching it in his huge paw, and stuffed it in his pocket.

"Can't. Can't tell him."

"Yeah. Why not?"

"It's really tragic. He's dead."

"That's right," Noodles added. "He's dead. He died."

"Yeah, what of?"

"Alcoholic."

The kid said, "In Kishnev, Poland."

"Then he don't need it no more, does he? So it's been requisitioned." He turned his back on the two boys and walked away, whistling and swinging his stick.

"What's that mean?" the kid asked Noodles. "Requi-what?"

"It means pinched. By him," Noodles answered. "At seven thirty-seven."

The cop swung around suddenly and pointed a finger at the two of them. "Just remember I got my eye on you two wise-asses."

The blond smiled and said under his breath so that only Noodles could hear, "I got my eye on you, too, cossack." He stepped back and bumped into the wagon, jarring the lamp, which would have fallen to the ground had not Noodles been quick enough to grab it.

A woman's voice called from a window high up. "Max!"

The blond kid looked up. "Yeah, Mom, what d'ya want?"

"Stop with the talk and bring up the furniture. You want it should be stolen? Who's that you're talking to?"

The boy, whose name Noodles now knew, called back to her as he once more picked up the crate, "My uncle."

Noodles grinned, picked up the camera with his free hand, and carrying it and the lamp, followed Max as he took the crate into the house.

CHAPTER
6

So far as Patsy knew, Peggy didn't have an old man. Of course she had one once, but he'd never seen no old geezer in the place, and he was pretty sure he'd heard around that Peggy lived alone with her mother. Unfortunately, he'd also heard that her mother was a pretty hard cookie. But at least it wasn't like she was a man and could knock him down or anything. Besides, he told himself, so far as anyone at the house was concerned he was only going to ask for Peggy, and if they asked him why he was asking for her, he was gonna say because he had a message for her from a girlfriend. Then, when they were alone, he'd show Peggy the food and tell her she could have the whole thing if she'd go somewhere in the building with him and let him do it to her.

He was pretty confident that she wouldn't say no, although not so confident that it would be so easy getting her alone in the hall. He'd never dealt with any girls before and certainly never dealt with their mothers. As he climbed the stairs toward the floor where Noodles and Peggy both lived, he hoped that he'd be lucky and her mother'd be out. Then he could go inside the apartment and they could use a regular bed or a sofa or something. Of course, then there was the chance her mother'd come home and catch them, or maybe there'd be an uncle or someone and he'd get the crap beaten out of him. Well, if that happened, the gang'd take care of the guy, whoever he was. Hell, Bugsy would personally see to it, he thought.

Unless Peggy was somehow related to Bugsy . . .

By the time he reached the right floor, Patsy was in a sweat. He peered down the hall, didn't see anyone, and for a moment was tempted to run away, but his penis had grown large in his pants just thinking about it and he decided he'd better do something, especially since Noodles knew he was coming over to see Peggy and would expect a full and truthful report.

He looked down at the waxed-paper package swinging daintily in his hand. After he passed Noodles' door, he shifted it behind his back. Peggy lived in the corner apartment. Timidly he pushed the doorbell and jumped back when he heard its loud ring, which seemed to echo throughout the building. He hoped no one was listening. Finally, when he was about to give up hope and slip away, the door opened a crack. A big beefy woman looked out at him. When she saw that it was only a boy, she opened the door wider, but not so wide that he could get in or even see beyond her.

"I thought maybe you were the collector. What d'ya want, kid?" The woman smelled faintly of soap.

"Good morning. Sorry to bother you. Peggy home?"

"Yeah, but she's takin' a bath."

"That's great. I mean, of course, I didn't mean— Would you mind being so kind as to tell her that I'm out here with a message and—"

"Yeah, sure. Hold your horses. She'll be a few minutes."

From inside he heard Peggy's voice cry

out, "C'mon, Ma, I'm all soapy. You said you'd bring some more water."

"Jesus!" the woman exclaimed, closing the door in Patsy's face.

He went and sat on the steps that led to the next landing. He could hear the noises of the building very clearly; he could even hear Peggy arguing with her mother. Someone came up the stairs below and went into an apartment. He wasn't sure in the gloom, but he thought maybe it was Noodles. He began to tap his foot in impatience, when he noticed the package in his hand.

A little piece of pastry and he was gonna get a little piece of something more than pastry. What the hell, he thought, she probably loves to do it. Probably if he didn't have the charlotte russe, she'd still do it. He sniffed the waxed paper in which the gooey confection was wrapped. A little glob of whipped cream was leaking out the side. He reached his finger down to push it back, but it wouldn't go, so he brought his finger to his mouth and licked it clean with his tongue.

What was taking her so long? Hell, she was only taking a bath. That took him about two minutes once a week. Well, she'd smell nice and she'd be nice and clean. He'd heard about what you could get from girls who weren't clean. If she gave *him* a dose, he'd bust her one right in the snoot.

He got up and moved around, but was afraid that if he made too much noise he'd call attention to himself. Maybe even get her mother mad and she wouldn't let Peggy go out. He sat down and looked at the paper. Just another taste. He really *was* hungry. He should have gotten two nickel ones. She'd never have known the difference. He reached his finger in and moved it around until he felt the wetness of the cream. After he had licked his finger clean, he noticed he had mused the package, spoiled its looks. Deciding to undo it and retie the string, he opened it up. It sure looked good. She wouldn't notice if he took just one bite.

It tasted even better with the pastry and powdered sugar mixed with the whipped cream. He gulped down the bite, stared at the remains. Now it looked lopsided. A bite from the other end to even it up. He hadn't realized how hungry he was, nor how delicious Gelly's pastry could be. Before he knew it, he had gulped down the whole thing.

Just then the door opened and Peggy came out, looking shiny and fresh, carrying a wicker basket full of laundry. She looked him over before she spoke.

"What do you want?" There was a little

annoyance in her voice, but curiosity, too, as though she already knew why he was hanging around.

"Me?"

"My ma said you were looking for me. I guess it was you. She said some guy had a message."

"Oh . . . yeah . . . well . . . no . . . you see, the guys told me—"

"What did the guys tell you?"

"Nothin'. Nothin' really."

"Yeah. Well, you tell the guys not to talk about things they don't know nothin' about. See?"

"Sure. I guess I'll be goin'." He stood up to let her pass with her wicker basket. "I'll come back some other time." When she had gone by him, he sat down again, lost in gloom. Maybe, he thought, if I ask her, she'd let me. It couldn't hurt to try.

He followed her up the stairs. On the next landing there was a window through which he could see the roof. Looking out, he heard the door open and close up above. Then he saw Peggy go out on the roof and reach up to a line that held a sheet and clothespins. But that wasn't what stopped him from following her. What stopped him was the man jumping from roof to roof. His movements were devious, as if he were determined that no one see him. The man caught sight of Peggy and waved. Then he leapt over to the roof where she was standing, and she finished hanging up the last sheet so that Patsy could see neither of them. It didn't matter, though. He knew what they were going to do. And he knew who the man was, too.

The man was Whitey the cop.

Patsy turned and dashed down the stairs, hoping that the footsteps he'd heard *had* belonged to Noodles and that his friend was at home in his apartment.

Pounding on the door, he cried out, "Noodles! Noodles!"

Except that while one is standing on them one is exposed to fresh air and sunlight (or soot, darkness, rain, or snow, as the case may be), tenement roofs have little to recommend them. They are covered with tar and layers of dirt; drainage is inadequate so there are often puddles that breed bugs and feed vermin; smoke pours from chimneys, thick and black; venturing too close to the edge can lead to loss of life, for there are no railings; they provide easy access for burglars; and illicit sex can be had without loved ones below being aware of what is taking place.

Illicit sex was what Whitey had in mind,

what he, in fact, had accomplished on several previous occasions with the heavy-chested and not overly fastidious Peggy. He was worried about it. After all, she was a minor and he was a cop. But she had been available for a very reasonable price—a few sweets. He had told himself that he wouldn't go back a second time, but he had. And a third. He had told himself that sooner or later someone would find out. But when no one complained after the first—or the second—or third—time, he showed up again, overconfident now.

That was why he was shocked and terrified, but not totally surprised, when the magnesium flash went off. He was lying on top of Peggy, who was lying on top of a pile of clean laundry, surrounded by already-drying sheets that offered a kind of wall-like protection; he was bare-assed and, at the moment, extremely red-faced.

A flock of pigeons who fed and defecated and made pigeon love on the roof were startled and fluttered away. Whitey was equally startled, but he had nowhere to fly.

He leaped up in terror, leaving a cringing, naked Peggy on a heap of laundry as Noodles called out, "Did you get it?"

At first Whitey thought that Noodles was

talking to him, asking a rather vulgar question. Then he heard Max's reply.

"I think his asshole blinked, but we got him."

When the stars finally cleared from his eyes, Whitey saw Noodles holding a magnesium flash, standing beside Max, who was looking over the top of the camera. A third kid—Patsy, Whitey thought his name was—stood behind them, grinning like a little ape. Whitey threw himself against the wall of the shed that formed the fourth side of his little love nest. His pants were around his ankles and he was exposed for all to see. As fast as he could, before they tried to take a picture of that, he pulled at the worn navy-blue pants that were shiny in seat and knees.

Max spoke again. "Nice goin', Fartface. And on duty, too. What d'ya think the sergeant'll say, and you supposed to be on the street stealing apples from pushcarts?"

Whitey's shorts were twisted in the blues and he was having a hard time getting himself covered while still trying to regain a little composure. He decided to brazen it out, treat it like a joke until he could get the film. Then he'd take care of the little Jew bastards.

"I gotta admit it, you caught me with me pants down that time, boys."

Noodles corrected him. "We caught you with your schmuck up the tochis of a minor."

"More like a putz," Max amended, "from what I can see."

Peggy, not even modest enough to cover her bare breasts and middle, sat up and began to laugh.

Max pulled the plate from the camera and handed it to Patsy. "Scram," he said, "put this someplace safe. Someplace where—"

"Hold on," Whitey said, starting after Patsy despite his twisted trousers. But Patsy, moving like a rat being chased by a terrier, was already on his way down the stairs. When Whitey realized he wasn't going to have a chance of catching Patsy, he stopped and tried to act nonchalant.

"Now, what are you gonna do with that plate? Hell, it don't mean nothin'. Probably out of focus. C'mon, one ass looks like another. No one's gonna know it's me, so why don't you forget it. What're you gonna do with it?"

Noodles looked around, then responded vaguely, as if it were a matter of complete indifference to him, "Depends. What time is it, Max?"

Max walked over to Whitey and said, "It's time we got our watch back." He reached into Whitey's tunic, grabbed the gold chain, and pulled it and the watch slowly toward him, not taking his eyes off Whitey.

"Okay, boys," he said, trying to make best of it, "we're even."

Max had the watch, which he put into his own pants pocket. "The hell we are," he said.

"You'll be collecting your pension," Noodles added, "before we're even."

Seeing they were serious, Whitey said evenly, "Okay, what do you boys want?" He finally got his pants straightened out and began to button the fly.

Max and Noodles, at the same time, began to unbutton theirs.

"I'm serious, boys. What else'll you be wantin' for that plate?"

Max said, "Noodles was telling me about somebody called Bugsy. Seems he's the boss of the neighborhood, thanks to you."

Noodles went to where Peggy was sitting and pulled the sheet down, hiding them from view.

"Meaning what?"

"Meaning he pays you off."

Peggy's voice called out, "What's the rush? Take it easy."

Ignoring this, Max continued, "Why does Bugsy pay you off? What do ya do for him?"

Whitey replied, "Well, maybe I'm closing an eye for him now and then."

Again they could hear Peggy's voice mixed with groans coming from Noodles. "Enjoy it, stupe. Don't be in such a— What did I tell you? Easy come, easy go."

"From now on," Max told Whitey, "you're closing an eye for us."

"Why? What are you gonna be up to?"

Noodles reappeared, red in the face, looking ruffled but pleased with himself. Max pointed to him and said, "He'll tell you. I got a little business with Peggy."

As he disappeared behind the sheet, Noodles said, "Me, him, Patsy, and Cockeye are working together. We're takin' over."

"You're loony. You're just kids. I may not think much of you, but I don't want be identifyin' you down at the city morgue. Bugsy'll flatten you. He'll put you away. I can't afford that. I won't put up with any rough stuff in my precinct."

"You'll put up—and you'll shut up. You hear nothin' and you see nothin', just like with Bugsy."

Max swore from behind the sheet. "*Gevalt*—already!"

"Don't get all fartootst! It can happen the first time. Come on inside."

"It's them two talkin' out there."

Noodles laughed and said to Whitey,

96

"You're spoilin' the mood. We understand each other—so beat it, copper."

Max came out from behind the laundry curtain. "Before you go, as a gesture of goodwill, you're paying Peggy—for us."

"Sure, kid, anything you say." Whitey took a bill from his pants pocket, which Noodles promptly grabbed.

"Here I come, Peggy, ready for more. I can't believe it. My first time, and a mick cop is paying for it."

Peggy laughed.

"He'll never get it up," Whitey said.

"Sure he will, Fartface. He's got all the balls in the world. That's why we're partners. Got a smoke?"

C H A P T E R

7

It was Friday night and the streets were crowded. Merchants who were closing their shops before sundown in order to meet the requirements of their religion were preparing themselves to attend services at the synagogue. Many of the men were wearing yarmulkes on their heads, some of them carried long tallithsim. Women carried babies wrapped in shawls; they themselves wore shawls and babushkas. Everyone was dressed in his or her best, no matter how poor that best might be, no matter how worn and shoddy the finery.

Noodles, too, was in the street, but he was

neither dressed for services, wearing a yarmulke, nor headed in the direction of the synagogue. He was following someone. The someone walked nimbly and quickly, her braid bouncing behind her, her ballet shoes tied together and slung over her shoulder. Her body was slim, and she moved wraithlike through the crowd, her form almost indistinct in the fading light. She seemed at times to disappear, to be swallowed up by the throng, yet Noodles always found her again, always stayed just far enough behind so that she wouldn't notice him, yet close enough to be able to tell if she changed direction.

All at once he stopped and ducked into a doorway. She had reached the delicatessen just as her father and brother were about to leave. The men of her family were on their way to services, dressed accordingly. They exchanged a few words, then she took the key her father offered her and let herself in the side door as Gelly and Fat Moe stepped off the curb and into the stream of people. When he was sure they were not going to turn back, Noodles left his hiding place and slipped into the alley after her.

His heart crowded his Adam's apple as he approached the side door. He couldn't believe his luck when he saw that it was ajar. Pushing it open a little wider, he peered inside, then looked around to make sure that no one was watching. He stepped inside, closing the door softly behind him, and tiptoed into the empty lunchroom, but she wasn't in sight. From beyond a door he could hear the victrola being wound up, its crank squeaking at each complete turn. Suddenly, music filled the air. The tune was one he had heard before, one that he had grown to love: "Amapola."

Moving on cat's feet, he approached the door to the bathroom, and just as he had done previously, he piled up several crates so that he would be able to peek through the grating. At first he couldn't see anything, but even when his eyes adjusted, the room, despite the music, seemed to be empty.

"Get down off of there, roach." Her voice pierced through him like a poisoned arrow, and he fell backward, tumbling to the floor, bringing the wooden crates down on top of him. When he looked up, she was standing there, hands on her still-boyish hips, looking down at him and laughing.

"That record is like Ex-Lax. Every time I put it on the victrola, you end up having to go to the bathroom."

Attempting to collect his dignity as well as his wits, Noodles climbed awkwardly out of the pile of crates. Deborah had already disappeared and he followed her back to the lunchroom. She glanced over her shoulder, then went into the apartment. He wasn't sure if he was supposed to follow. He wanted to do so very much, but he was still in awe of her; she was so unlike the other girls he knew. Peggy, for instance.

Chickening out, he sat on one of the counter stools, trying to appear nonchalant.

Finally she returned, asking, "What are you doing?"

Ignoring her, he fished a nickel from his pocket and flipped it onto the counter. "Gimme a beer," he said grandly.

"Huh! We're closed, for one thing. And I don't wait on people, for another. Besides, nice people don't drink on Pesach. They go to the synagogue."

"Oh, yeah? Then what are you doin' here?" There, he thought, he had her.

"Somebody's got to keep an eye on the place. Otherwise those little thieves out there, they could come right into your house, and who knows what would happen."

"Especially if you leave the door open." He had her there and he knew it.

Deborah flounced out of the room. He could hear her lift the needle from the record. Slowly he got up and went to the doorway. When he looked in, he could see her waiting for him by the gramophone. Even so, he hesitated.

Quite suddenly she said, "You can pray here just as well as in the synagogue. It's the same difference. It's what's in your heart that counts." She turned to one of the orange crates that served as tables and picked up a large volume that Noodles recognized at once as a Bible.

"Come on over here and sit down." It was half-request, half-command. Either way he was not about to refuse whatever she had to offer. When he was seated on the floor, she opend the book to a well-thumbed page and started to read, now and then looking up at him.

"Listen. 'My beloved is white and ruddy. His skin is as the fine gold, his cheeks are as a bed of spices . . .'" Lowering the book and staring at his neck she added, "Even though he hasn't washed since last December."

Noodles looked shamefully away, then felt himself begin to harden in his trousers. His face reddened, but she was speaking again, reading to him—to him!—in a low voice.

"'His eyes are as the eyes of doves, his body as bright as ivory, his legs are as pillars of marble . . .'"

Again she stopped and looked down at, he

was sure, his crotch. "In pants so dirty they stand by themselves."

Before he could move or say anything, she went back to her reading. " 'He is altogether lovable . . .' " then her voice turned bitterly sarcastic as she added, "But he'll always be a two-bit punk, so he'll never be my sweetheart. What a shame! And he'll never get what he wants more than anything in the world, no matter how hard he tries."

She had moved close to him, her voice intense, her body trembling, willing. Impetuously he stood up, pulled her close, smothering her mouth with awkward, brutal kisses. He could feel her heart beating, feel her immature breasts pressed against his chest. For a moment he thought they were going to tumble to the floor, then she regained her composure and pushed away saying, "Someone's there. Watching." He looked toward heaven, then realized she was talking about the grate.

Releasing her, he ran out of the room, through the deli, and into the john. The door was open and it was clearly empty. When he came out, she was standing back near the counter and on her face was a look he had never seen before on a girl, the look of absolute certainty, of being totally in control, of knowing that she had the upper hand and would always have it. He would have slapped her face for leading him on if he hadn't heard a familiar whistle and his name being called from out in the alley.

He stopped short and said to her, "There ain't nobody. How could there be. You knew that." The whistle again.

He could hear Max's voice, calling him. "Noodles!" How the hell did Max know where to find him? Another whistle, its intensity suggesting urgency.

"It's Max," he said.

"Spying on us."

The voice was louder, right outside the door. "Noodles!"

Noodles hesitated, looking at Deborah and the apartment beyond. Did she want him to stay? If he did, would she . . . ?

She must have read his mind, for, her voice a mixture of sarcasm and challenge, she looked him straight in the eye as she said, "Go on, run. Your mother's calling you. Go on, before something happens to you."

"I'm just gonna . . . see what he wants. Maybe it's important. I'll be right back."

Max was standing in the alley, one foot on an upturned crate, polishing his shoe with a piece of newspaper.

"Hey," Noodles said, "what's up?"

"Yo." Max barely turned his head. He took

his foot down, replaced it with the other, and began polishing again.

"Was that you callin' me? Whistlin'?"

"Uh-huh."

"Been here long?"

"Nope."

"Were you in there . . . in Gelly's . . . ?"

Max tossed away the newspaper, brought his foot down, and said with a sneer, "You are one lousy kisser. Hey, don' get mad. I was tryin' to catch up with you, and then I seen you go in there after that ball-buster. Believe me, she's nothin' but a tease." Sensing that he had gone too far, Max changed the subject. "Hey, this is for the stuff from last night." He reached up, took off his cap, and removed a roll of bills from the sweatband. "Four bucks for the typewriter, six for the silverware. Shitsy Lipshitz wouldn't cough up any more. We gotta get somebody else. You know, if there's competition, the price goes up. Shitsy knows we ain' got no one else to go to 'cause that bastard Bugsy gave him the territory. Hey, what's the matter? You mad or somethin'? Do you want to divvy it up or don't you?"

Noodles turned back toward the deli. "Tomorrow. With the others." His voice was abrupt, angry.

"Wait a minute. I got somethin' else, too. I came to pick you up—"

"Not now. I can't come now."

"Listen, this is important." Max's voice grew excited. "The houses, the stores ... they're all empty. You know, everyone's in temple. We got our pick." When Noodles didn't respond, Max added, "Our pick ... and you pick that? There's always plenty of that around."

Noodles thought for a moment, torn because he wanted the money, but not as much as he wanted Deborah. The trouble was, was she really waiting for him to come back? Did she want him to? And if he did, would she just tease him, lead him on? She'd said he'd never make it with her. But he knew she wanted to, only ...

Max interrupted his thoughts. "Some partner I got." He started down the alley toward the street, calling back over his shoulder, "Have fun."

Noodles watched him go, or he wouldn't have seen four burly men he didn't know fill the space where the alley joined the street. With the four men was a fifth, whom he recognized at once. Two of the men ran past Max to the far end of the alley while the other two neatly pushed a cart across the entrance, effectively blocking the exit for

Noodles. Max was beyond the cart, on its safe side, but heedless of his own danger, he scrambled over the wagon and ran to Noodles' side.

"Looks like we're in for it, partner. I take it that creep who looks like a monkey is your friend, Bugsy."

"That's him."

"Yeah, he looks like a Bugsy."

The four men had closed in on them, and as Noodles pulled the knife from his pocket and flipped it open, they grabbed the two boys, twisting their arms behind their backs. The knife dropped to the ground and one of the men kicked it harmlessly out of the way.

Bugsy, not much taller than the boys, walked up to the now-helpless Max and Noodles. His mouth was slack, gaping open on the right-hand side, giving his half-smile a demonic look.

"Good evening, Noodles. Long time no see. Ain't you gonna innerduce me to your friend here? Okay, in that case, I'll innerduce myself." He reached into his pocket with his right hand and took out a set of brass knuckles, which he fitted over his hand.

" 'Scuse my glove." His fist drove viciously into Max's face. Blood spurted from the boy's nose and mouth.

"My name is Bugsy. You must be Max, the big-shot kid I been hearing so much about. The one that don't want no innerference from the cop on the block. I heard you had a lot to say, Max, but right now you seem pretty quiet to me. That's too bad. Nothin' I like more than a good conversation with an important man like yourself. You know, nothin' would make me happier than to continue this little talk we're havin', but I get tired easily. So I think I'll let my boys here talk to you two men of the world, you two punks who think you can muscle"—his voice had reached a high-pitched scream—"in on Bugsy!"

He stepped back and nodded to the four thugs. Each of the men had similar brass knuckles, which they fitted to their hands, and then, taking turns, they expertly and savagely beat Noodles and Max until they fell, bloody, to the ground. Then the men began to kick them mercilessly. Bugsy stood silently watching until he thought the boys had had enough and his message had been gotten across.

Delicately, Bugsy leaned down and poked Max, patting him down gently until he found what he was looking for, a wad of money stashed inside his shirt. He took it out, counted it, and took off two bills, which he dropped on the ground in front of Max. "Kids your age don't know how to take care of money. Besides, havin' too much gives you bad habits. You might start spending it on dames or booze or God-knows-what. Cigarettes maybe, and that would stunt your growth. I hope you understand what I'm sayin'. This is the cut I take from who works for me. Who don't work for me, I don' care, because he don't work. Period. Get me, punks? I'm the boss."

Max, staring at Bugsy with hatred, said through his bloody teeth, "I don't like bosses."

"Tough titty, kid. You don't like bosses, better you stayed in the Bronx."

"Better for you, too."

"Hey, you got me scared, kid." Bugsy aimed his foot directly into Max' stomach. The blow was so painful that Max began to vomit as he squirmed in agony.

Bugsy signaled his thugs to push the cart away from the alley exit, then he slowly walked away, leaving Max and Noodles groaning on the ground, writhing in pain, their faces bruised and cut and already beginning to swell.

Max sat up slowly, saying, "I'm gonna kill him. Someday soon I'm gonna get a chance to kill him and I'm gonna do it. I only hope I can make it slow so he knows it was me who done it, but the first chance I get—"

"Yeah, but right now it feels like he's killed us. If you feel as bad as I do."

"If you still wanna work for him, Noodles, go ahead. But I'm on my own. You can tell the other guys."

Noodles pulled himself up beside Max. "No. I don't think working for him would be much fun anymore. Besides, my grandfather used to say, 'Take big steps. You get there faster and it saves shoe leather.'"

Noodles tried to stand up, but his legs wouldn't hold him and he collapsed in a heap beside Max. "Ah! Shit! I hurt places I never knew you could hurt."

Crawling over to him, Max asked, "Can't you walk? I can."

"I don't think so, Max."

Getting to his feet, slowly and with a great deal of pain, Max reached down and offered his hand. "I'll help you home. Lean on me."

Noodles shook his head. "Not like this. My ma sees me like this she'd have a heart attack and then she'd have a fit and prob'ly work me over some more."

"Mine, too."

"Wait a minute," Noodles said, "I got an idea." Struggling to his knees, he crawled across the alley to the side entrance to Gelly's.

He started to push it open when he heard the key turn in the lock.

"Deborah! It's me, Noodles. We . . . I need . . . Open up, will ya?" He reached up and hit his fist as hard as he could on the door.

Standing on the other side, her face white with terror and sadness, but stern with resolve, Deborah turned away and went back to her practice room, where she closed the door and began to crank the victrola.

CHAPTER
8

The skyline of Lower Manhattan is one of the most beautiful views in the world. Tall, narrow buildings dot the pie-shaped area, majestic sentinels on guard against invaders from beyond. Two rivers converge at the tip of the pie and then spill toward the ocean, washing the shores of Brooklyn along the way. Three bridges, monuments in iron, their zigzagged grillwork creating patterns of endless variation, join the island of Manhattan with Brooklyn, carrying people and goods back and forth twenty-four hours a day. The bridges are themselves works of art as well as necessities of travel and commerce, and the fact that they had been built and stand suspended across the East River is near to being miraculous. From atop the grandest of these spans, the Brooklyn Bridge, the view of Lower Manhattan and its waterfront is almost a religious experience.

However, closer examination of the waterfront area where ships from all over the world are berthed after belching forth their cargo—coffee and bananas from South America, rubber from Southeast Asia, wool and wine from Europe—shows decay, dilapidation, rust, and ruin. This, too, is the waterfront. Slums, not nearly so invisible from close up, seem dwarfed by the large commercial buildings. These slums go right to the water's edge.

Across the river, in Brooklyn, the waterfront decay is worse; the slums more numerous and ugly. Only the view is better. For from Manhattan you can see only the sprawling, flatlands of Brooklyn, but from Brooklyn you can see Lower Manhattan and you can believe, however foolishly, that there is a chance for a better life.

The men working in Brooklyn rarely look up, rarely look across to the city. In factories they keep their eyes on the machines, grateful that they are working and earning a wage that somehow is never quite enough to feed and clothe their families.

A car pulld up outside of one of these factories, a printing plant, and a heavyset man named Al got out. He was not dressed like a typical worker: he wore a suit and tie, as befitted his status as an owner of the plant. The plant did more than produce large rolls of newsprint, however, but Al's enterprise could not be totally condemned, for these were times when many men held down more than one job. And Al's second business was considerably more profitable than the printing presses.

He mounted a stairway and walked through the dirty aisles, oblivious to the steady hum of the machinery and the silent nods of the ink-smeared employees. Looking up to a catwalk where the foreman was overseeing the work, Al called out above the roar, "That stuff ready for the *Globe*?"

"They're loading it now."

Al nodded his approval, pleased that everything was going according to schedule. He went to a cupboard built along one of the walls and opened a door, as if he might be going to hang up his coat, but instead he walked into the cupboard, closing the door behind him. Inside the door was a narrow stairway leading down to a room filled with more equipment, the kind of equipment necessary for his second business: stills, vats, bottling machines, a network of tubing, packing cases of empty bottles, stacks of full ones now labeled. Al and his brothers were also in the business of brewing, bottling, and distributing illegal alcoholic beverages: they made and sold bootleg booze.

A trapdoor in the middle of the floor was open, giving way to the river below—a safe, secure, hidden means of convenient transportation from the stills to the big Manhattan markets. Several men, sweating as they worked, were busy loading crates of bottles into a motorboat that bobbed in the water below. This was the "stuff for the *Globe*" that Al had asked about.

Nearby, to Al's surprise and annoyance, his two younger brothers, Freddie and Gianni, impressive in their black sharkskin suits and sparkling diamond pinky rings, were in a serious discussion with five kids. The five were obviously still youngsters, but they had a mature and worldly-wise look about them. Four of them were getting close to the age when, if arrested, they would not be sent to a juvenile court, and if convicted, they might be sent to a state prison, but they were considerably younger than any of the men in the hidden still.

"What the fuck is this, a kindergarten?" he called over to them.

Surprised, the others turned and looked at him. Freddie laughed, turned his back on the boys, and winked at his older brother. "Sssh! Can't you see we're busy with the big boys today."

"Hell, yes," Gianni added. "They want to work for us. Wha' d'ya think, Al, take 'em on as torpedoes?"

Max, the spokesman for the group, a few years older and even more sure of himself, now dressed in a way that attempted to add maturity. He addressed Al. "That's right. Doin' what Bugsy does. We want his job."

Freddie laughed. "Get this kid, Al. A regular comedian, huh?"

Dominic, eager perhaps to play on ethnic concerns, tried to show he was one of the Family by affecting a bogus Italian-immigrant accent. "Eh, Capuano, isa da besta proteck you eva gonna get, son-a-da-bitch, isa true."

"Fuck off, kid. I got no time for this shit. Who the hell do you punks think you are? What the fuck you gonna protect? Go protect your mother's ass, she's hustlin' on the street."

His brothers laughed.

Max shrugged, turned to the others, and

said, "Come on, let's go. Noodles, we'll peddle your invention to someone else."

"Hey, Al," Freddie said, "what the hell, listen to what the ass-hole kids have to say. They got nothin' to sell, jus' jerkin' us around, we pitch 'em in the river, huh?"

"Okay, kid," Al said to Max after thinking it over, "you got one minute. Make it good or you'll get the first bath you had in a month."

Ignoring the threat, Max said, "You ship your stuff by the river, right?"

"What the hell you think you're standing over? Some of it, we do, yeah."

"And when you get stopped by the customs boats or the coast guard, you gotta throw the cases overboard."

"Whicha means," Dominic chimed in, "datta you lose-a da whole-a shipment."

"Cut the shit, kid," Al said. To Max, he added, "You got half a minute left."

Noodles said, "For ten percent we'll save it all for you."

Gianni giggled. "How? You got a submarine?"

Dominic folded his arms across his chest and said, "We got salt."

"You got what?" Freddie could see Al was getting annoyed and he worried when Al got annoyed. "Salt? I think you kids better get out of here fast."

Patsy, silent until now, added mysteriously, "Me and the guys are old salts."

"In a minute you're gonna be river rats," Al snarled.

Cockeye added, "But we need about three tons of salt per shipment. Give or take."

Al, really pissed now, turned to his brothers. "These little punks are pullin' our pricks."

"What the fuck's with all this salt?" Fred asked. Now he was worried Al was mad at him for even talking to this cocky bunch of kids.

Max smiled triumphantly and, pointing to Noodles' head, said, "We got salt on our Noodles! Show him, partner."

Noodles opened an old pencil box he was holding and took out a miniature crate tied to a little sack and a piece of cork. He looked at the blank faces of the three brothers, tapped the sack, and said, "This is full of salt."

"Yeah, and you're full of shit." Al moved menacingly forward.

Noodles went to one of the tanks and calmly dropped the contraption in, and it promptly sank to the bottom. The Capuano brothers came over to the tank and peered down.

"So?" Al said.

"Keep-a you shirt on, Capuano."

"Yeah," Noodles said. "We gotta wait for the salt to dissolve."

Ribbons of fog hovered over the broad sweep of the merging rivers. The light of dawn was barely discernible through the mist. Deep-throated foghorns bellowed in the distance, calling secret messages to one another. A few lights winked from the nearby city, but for all practical purposes the water remained shrouded by mist and darkness.

Two rowboats, abreast of each other, bobbed uncertainly in the water. Two boys sat in one, Max and Noodles; in the other huddled Patsy, Cockeye, and Dominic. All five stared anxiously into the black waters of the East River, where it swept around the curve of Brooklyn, a section of water aptly named the Narrows. Patches of oil, mementos from passing ships, made the ripples glisten.

They were nervous, as much because they were not used to being in boats and fearful of the heavy river traffic as because they worried that their experiment done in washtubs might not pass the much more rigorous test of the real world. Perhaps because of this, Cockeye withdrew his flute from his sleeve and played a brave little tune.

As if summoned by the song, a red balloon

popped out of the water only a few yards from where they were anchored.

Patsy saw it first. "There's one," he shouted, his voice echoing across the water and momentarily drowning out the foghorns.

A few feet away, in a different direction, a yellow balloon burst forth from the inky depths. Dominic spotted it and his shout was even louder than Patsy's. "There's another."

All of a sudden the water around the two rowboats seemed to be filled with balloons. The screams of joy and triumph from the boats were enough to frighten the soaring gulls that had hovered above, mistakenly believing them to be fishermen who would be throwing unused bait over the side.

Max and Noodles stood in their bobbing boat, their arms about each other, executing a little dance of pleasure, newfound power, and relief that they hadn't failed. Not being sailors, they didn't realize that water reacted differently than land to such exuberance, and before they could recover, they found themselves pitched into the river, where their two darkly wet heads bobbed among their precious balloons.

Noodles surfaced first and looked around for Max. The three boys in the other boat were busy hauling in crates from where their markers had appeared. They were clearly unaware that Noodles and Max had fallen into the swift-moving current.

Hoisting himself over the side of the boat, Noodles looked around for Max. Now worried, he anxiously scanned the water near the boat.

"Max!" he called out. "Max!"

When there was no response, he kicked off his shoes and dove back into the chilly water, swimming beneath the rowboat and the crates rising with their balloons. He could see garbage, refuse of all kinds, the crates, the bottom of their boat as well as the other, but there was no sign of Max.

At last, his lungs bursting for air, he shot back up to the surface. Gasping and terrified, he tried to call out to the others. For a moment he thought he would be swept away, too, until his hand caught the edge of the boat and he pulled himself partway up, only to be met by Max's grinning face, peering down over the gunwhale, mocking him.

"My, my, this river sure has a lot of weird things floating in. What's the matter, Noodles? Lose something?"

"Bastard."

"But what would you do without me?"

For an answer, Noodles ducked his head and brought it back up quickly, spitting a mouthful of dirty East River water right into Max's face.

The desolation of a train station at four o'clock in the morning is complete. A single voice, if it were to cry out, would reverberate to sky-high ceilings and float eerily down cavernous halls, echoing across granite and marble canyons before dying, unheard, unanswered. The train engines are silent, asleep, waiting for daybreak and the new onslaught of travelers; the workers, too, are gone, home in bed resting their weary bodies; and the public, the people who depend on the trains to move them through the city, secure that the station and the trains will be there when they are needed, are at home slumbering, uncaring.

An ideal time for criminal mischief, whether it be murder or conspiracy. That was why the five young men standing together by the door of a locker, bundled in handsome new overcoats, wearing shiny shoes and smart hats perched uncomfortably on heads unused to such adornment, were unconcerned that they might be noticed as they joined hands in a solemn pact. The hands so joined rested on a straw suitcase.

Way off in the distance a train coughed

once or twice, then rumbled steadily down the track, heading out of the station until it could no longer be heard.

Max steadied the suitcase with his free hand as he spoke, his voice taking on the intonation of a funeral orator.

"From here on we establish the shared funds of the whole gang. They belong to all of us together and to none of us alone. And we solemnly swear to put in fifty percent of everything we make. The other fifty to be divided equally, ten percent each. Agreed?"

In unison the others answered, "Agreed!"

They removed their hands from the suitcase and Max picked it up and started to push it into the locker. But before he could finish this maneuver, Dominic stopped him.

"Max? Please, huh, I wanna take another peek."

Max shrugged, looked at the others, and they all nodded. He brought the suitcase back and opened it. Dominic, followed by the others, peered inside. There were stacks of green bills, neatly bundled, a considerable sum. Still, what was there didn't fill but a small portion of the case.

Dominic sighed. Max slammed the lid shut, flipped the snaps, shoved Dom aside, put the suitcase in the locker, and closed the door. He removed the key after twisting the lock and held it up before the others.

"This goes to Fat Moe," he said. "But we don't say what it's for. And he gives it back only when we're all together or else he knows we're all dead except one of us, then he can give it to that one person. Agreed?"

Again they agreed. Max pocketed the key and together the five musketeers marched out of the station and into the life of the city, ready to conquer anything and anyone who stood in their way.

They came upon the first obstacle much sooner than they expected, only a few blocks from the station. Happy as larks, the five young men strode outside into the winter wind that whipped their new coats tight against the calves of their legs. Dominic, to keep warm, began a little tap dance that carried him down the street some distance ahead of the others. He turned the corner, leaving his friends behind, but reappeared almost at once, his lighthearted, rhythmic dance turning into a frantic race as he sped back to where they were gathered.

"Bugsy's coming," he hollered. "Run!"

A shot rang out, then another, as the boys broke for cover. Noodles dropped behind a parked car. As he turned to see what had happened to the others, he saw Dominic slide across several yards of icy pavement, moving like a skater out of control, then fall beside the car, a look of puzzled amazement on his young face.

Almost apologetically he said, "Noodles, I slipped."

Before Noodles could reply, Dominic was dead.

In the middle of the street, a revolver in his hand, Bugsy surveyed the scene. Seeing no one, he took a couple of tentative steps forward.

Like a cat Noodles was out from behind the car, his knife open and ready. Bugsy fired, but the shot went wild and Noodles was on him, ramming the shiv into Bugsy's stomach, then ripping it upward. Noodles pulled the blade out and, like a madman, drove it home again, cursing in grief and rage.

As Max ran out from his hiding place to help Noodles, two mounted policemen, clubs in hand, appeared on the scene. One of them swung at Noodles, dealing him a glancing blow on the head, and Noodles lost his balance.

He screamed out at the cop, "Yentzer! Schmuck!"

Max stood frozen as one of the cops dismounted and grabbed for Noodles, who, with blood running into his eyes from the cut on his head, struck out blindly, stabbing the cop in the chest. The second cop grabbed Noodles from behind and bashed him savagely on the head. The knife slipped from his grasp and Noodles slumped to the ground.

The trial was short, the sentence long, but not as long as it might have been. Noodles went for a visit upstate, to a vast gray prison.

On the day he was delivered over to the tender mercies of the state, Max, Patsy and Cockeye stood, like little lost sheep, outside the prison gates. A van moved to the entrance and stopped, waiting for the gates to slowly open. Noodles, handcuffed between two guards in the van, saw his friends standing there and jumped up, waving to them with his free hand.

The van started up, and Fat Moe, puffing as usual, ran to the boys, hoping that he was not too late to catch at least a glimpse of Noodles. When the wagon was inside the gate, it stopped. The four boys, stunned and motionless, looked at the blank gray walls and the pitiless arch on which the gates hung. Noodles continued to peer out from the back of the van as the huge iron bars of the gates slowly swung shut, separating him from his friends and the world he had vowed to conquer. Almost involuntarily, he started forward, and the guards laughed. The gate clanged shut, and he heard the latch slide home.

CHAPTER
9

1968

The bars of the cemetery gate swung open to reveal beautifully manicured lawns. Beyond were rows and rows of crypts and gravestones. Noodles walked forward until he came to the entrance of the tomb he sought. A Star of David, freshly polished and shiny, was bolted to the stone just above a brass plate that bore a biblical inscription.

> YOUR MEN WILL FALL BY THE SWORD,
> YOUR HEROES IN THE FIGHT.
> Isaiah, 3:25

Doors of heavy bronze were set in the white marble building. All around were flower beds as far as the eye could see, and blooming green shrubs encircled and hugged the tomb. Towering trees, their branches barely moving in the breeze, shaded the perfect lawn and buildings, giving the whole place a sense of peace and serenity. A nice place, perhaps, to live in, but hardly worth dying for.

A gardener, an old man with white hair and the strong bronze coloring of someone who has spent most his life working in the outdoors, stood respectfully a few feet from Noodles.

"You want to go in?" the man asked. When Noodles nodded, the man inquired, "Are you a relative?"

"An uncle." Noodles took out his wallet and pressed a bill into the man's hand. The money disappeared into a deep pocket before the gardener opened the bronze doors. He nodded at Noodles to enter.

Giving the door a hesitant push, Noodles started forward, only to stop when he heard the music filling the tomb. Music he hadn't heard in years—over thirty, in fact—the music of the flute, playing the sprightly little anthem that Cockeye had so often played. He looked up at the two loudspeakers on the ceiling and realized he was hearing some sort of recording, triggered to play when the doors opened. Knowing this, however, didn't relieve the unsettled feeling he had that he was being led on, watched, set up.

The walls of the tomb were gray marble, as shiny as a mirror. Bare and yet elegant, they were ornamented with three names and three dates etched in bronze:

MAXIMILIAN BERCOVICZ 1908–1933

PATRICK GOLDBERG 1909–1933

PHILIP STEIN 1909–1933

Drawn by the names, yet even more disturbed, Noodles moved into the tomb as the music continued to play, the same theme over and over again. His uneasiness became so great that he finally stepped in all the way and closed the door, stopping the music. As he did so, his gaze fell on a side wall of the tomb where a little tablet, tucked out of the way, almost as if it were an afterthought, sat in the wall. It, too, was inscribed:

ERECTED TO THEIR EVERLASTING MEMORY
BY THEIR FRIEND AND BROTHER
DAVID AARONSON—"NOODLES" 1967

Noodles turned pale. He stared at the plaque, reading it over and over again. He felt he was going to faint, but then a light, clinking sound, as though there were a single wind chime somewhere in the building, drew his attention. Moving a little closer to the inscription, he saw that something was hanging from the "D" in "NOODLES," and that it was rattling in the light breeze that was passing through the crypt. He reached out and took it in his hand. It was a key made of some sort of cheap metal—a key that was numbered, obviously to a locker in a railroad station.

Of course it was the same station; it had to be. Otherwise he wouldn't know where to begin to look. His memory wasn't good enough to tell him if it were the same locker or not, but it wouldn't have surprised him if it were. The place even looked pretty much the same. There was neon now, and the posters were different, but the layout hadn't changed. It smelled worse, of that he was sure. And there was a different kind of bum, now. Young, with long hair, on drugs. Quite a few of them around.

He inserted the key in the lock and opened the door, stepping back warily as he did so, almost as if he expected a bomb to go off. Inside was an old straw suitcase. And the building was, except for the rushing sounds of subway trains from beneath him, eerily silent. He opened the suitcase.

The contents were arranged in neat little bundles, carefully stacked, divided, and bound, that filled the suitcase to the top. One of the paper bands had a message typed on it. Noodles strained his eyes to read it.

"Advance payment for your next job."

Noodles slowly closed the case and lugged it from the station. The streets were empty, or seemed so; although it was still daylight, there was not a soul in sight. He was in a section of town where it was better not to be alone after dark. Especially with a suitcase containing a million dollars, give or take. The piers that supported the Elevated suddenly seemed like a forest of trees behind which lurked beasts of prey. A perfect spot for a mugging, he thought.

A taxi passed by. Noodles waved, but the driver kept on going, increasing his speed as he passed. Noodles began to walk, feeling his body getting warm with nervous perspiration. The knuckles of his hand were white from the tight grip he had on the suitcase. He gulped for air. Behind him he heard a high whine and a whistle. Turning, he was prepared for anything. Anything, that is, but the Frisbee, launched by an unseen hand, that skimmed his head as he ducked, and passed on. It was more frightening in its sudden appearance and unearthly movement than any real danger. He started to run.

Everywhere there were hands.

And bars. The Elevated superstructure, crisscrossing the way it did, made him think of bars. Prison bars.

C H A P T E R
10

1932

A hand reached out and grabbed the suitcase. The prison gates slammed behind him with finality.

"Max!"

Max reached to take Noodles' cheap suitcase from him as they looked at each other, noting the differences.

Six years was a long time.

"Noodles!"

Although both young men had matured over the years, it was Max who had changed the most. He was flashily dressed now, and

135

chomping on a big cigar, whereas Noodles was wearing the same cheap coat and shirt he had gone in with, neither of which quite fit.

Doffing his fedora and bowing from the waist, Max said, "Let me help you, sir."

Noodles was too overwhelmed to speak, but he followed Max across the road to where a majestic black hearse stood. Suddenly Noodles collected his wits and laughed, grabbing Max by the arm. Max dropped the suitcase as he turned around, and the two friends, longing to embrace, stood embarrassed, looking at each other, overcome by the strength of their feelings.

"How are you, Uncle? You're looking pretty good. At least they didn't starve you."

"You're certainly lookin' better."

"Yeah, how 'bout this." Max spun around, showing himself off, clowning to hide what he truly felt. "Hot stuff, huh? Makes the ladies pant, believe me."

He threw away his half-smoked cigar, unrolled a newspaper, and placed it sheet by sheet from Noodles' feet to the door of the hearse, as though he were laying down a red carpet for visiting royalty.

Noodles, nonplussed by the open coffin he could see through black velvet curtains at the window, hesitated.

Max said, "Your limousine is waiting."

"We pick up and deliver now, huh?"

"We own the company. It's a good cover and it pays off. Believe me, nothin' I do doesn't pay off."

"My ma wrote me you'd taken up body-snatching." He paused before he added softly, "And about everything you did for my family."

Tossing Noodles' suitcase beside the driver's seat, Max said, "Forget it. It's your dough. I got it all down in black and white in the company books." He pointed to the side of the hearse. "What do you think of our slogan? 'Why Go on Living When We Can Bury You for Forty-nine Fifty? Bercovicz and Company.' Cute, huh? You're the company. You, Patsy, and Cockeye. Gravediggers—and equal partners." Before noodles could say anything, Max opened the rear doors of the hearse. "But enough of this. We got a rush job. Business before pleasure."

Climbing inside, he beckoned Noodles to follow.

When Noodles had clambored in, Max got down to business. "A sudden death. A fuckin' tragedy." He pointed to the open coffin. A beautiful girl lay inside, covered to the chin by a purple sheet. "Nineteen years old." Pulling the sheet away, Max revealed her naked body. Her firm young breasts, with hardened nipples, seemed to reach up to the two young men, beckoning them.

"Too bad." Noodles sighed. "That's a beautiful plate of cold meat."

Max shook his head. "You don't get many like this. Took an overdose. It was a pleasure to get her ready. A real great stiff."

As Max gazed down at her, the girl opened her eyes, and her hand darted out and grabbed Noodles' crotch as she said, "And ready for another."

Max giggled, jumping up and down in the hearse in wild-eyed excitement. "Go ahead, Noodles, pump a little life into her. You didn't turn pansy in there, did you?"

For an answer Noodles started to strip off his clothes. Before Max could even shut the door, he had thrown himself on the girl, groaning with anticipation. Still laughing, Max climbed into the driver's seat. As the hearse started to pull away, a man who had been passing by stopped to stare at the tangle of writhing limbs inside the coffin.

Max leaned his head out the window and yelled to the man, "Turning over in the grave. Nobody believes it, but they do it every time." He drove off, leaving the man standing there, gaping, in a cloud of dust.

By the time the hearse reached its destination it was night. The old facade of Gelly's had been modernized to go with the changing times as well as the changed ownership. The sign now read FAT MOE'S, and the windows were newly scrubbed, reflecting street lamps in their shiny glass. There were no lights on inside, however, and the street itself was quiet.

Max climbed out, went around to the back, and opened the door. Noodles sat there, wearing a pleased look on his face. Slowly the girl got out of the back, her voluptuous body now clothed in a tight-fitting dress that not only outlined her figure but showed that it was quivering from the experience.

In a tiny little voice she said to Max, "Don't worry. Pansy he ain't."

Max grinned at her. "Good girl. Just what the doctor ordered. Hey," he added, handing her some bills, "don't you want a shot of something?"

"No, thanks, I'm full up." She walked away into the darkness, her body still shaking.

Noodles, still beaming as he tidied his hair with a pocket comb, stepped down and looked around, first at the street, then at what had once been an old deli.

"We call it Fat Moe's, but it belongs to us.

Moe's just a front. You gotta have ways to spend your money without nobody knowin' what's goin' on. We took over from Gelly in twenty-nine. This way we're still in the old neighborhood. It's safer. Know who your friends are. Smart, huh?"

They went to the window outside the lunchroom. So far as Noodles could see, the only additions to what was once Gelly's and was now called Fat Moe's were a couple of pool tables and a glass case that displayed cigarette packages. Almost all of the lights were out. The place was empty of customers; only a cook, scouring the range, and a waiter, stacking chairs so that he could mop the floor, were to be seen.

"Looks about the same. The whole neighborhood does. Nothing changes, I guess. Not in six years."

"Plenty has changed, believe me, Noodles." Max took him by the arm and dragged him into the side alley.

"Where we goin'?" Noodles asked, wary.

Bubbling with excitement, Max replied, "A place that never closes."

The first thing that Noodles noticed in the alley was a stream of fancy cars: some parked, some heading in, and some heading out of a garage at the alley's far end. Elegant people, many in evening wear, were getting in and out of the cars. They seemed to be in constant motion, either climbing or descending the wrought-iron stairway to a small door at the top.

"Where they going?" Noodles asked.

Smugly, with a smile as wide as his face, Max replied, "Our place. We've got the hottest spot in town. They come here to slum. But they spend big bucks, partner. And remember what I said, 'Our place.' "

Max pushed Noodles into a freight elevator, and when the doors opened, he was assaulted by a blare of jazz, shrill voices competing for attention, bright lights of many colors, and scores of well-dressed people everywhere, a classy-looking group in what had once been the back room of a deli and was now clearly a classy-looking speakeasy.

People were dancing and laughing and talking at a decibel level so high that Noodles, used to the dark look and dark sound of prison, was stunned into wide-eyed silence. Max, enjoying his friend's reaction, yelled in Noodles' ear, "This is the real Fat Moe's."

Noodles managed a smile. "Where are . . . ?"

As if on cue, Patsy and Cockeye plowed through the crowd and threw their arms around him.

"Patsy! Cockeye!"

"Noodles!"

Breaking free, Patsy yelled, "How 'bout a toast, for Chrissakes!"

Cockeye pulled his flute from his pocket and began to play his favorite tune, as Patsy went to the radiator on the wall, next to which stood a table holding dozens of teacups. Patsy took some cups, filled them from the radiator valve, and once they were filled, passed them to a waiter who, in turn, passed the full cups to Noodles, Max, and the others.

Winking, Patsy said, "Scotch heating. Really keeps you warm."

"And rich," Cockeye added, "at a buck a cup."

As he sipped the raw hootch, Noodles seemed to get control of all of his senses, and he started filtering his impressions to his brain, which had suddenly regained its business sense. "How much it cost us?" he asked.

"A dime—including overhead," was Max's excited reply.

Noodles let out a long whistle of delight, and then suddenly he was overwhelmed by the weight of a weeping whale that beached itself in his arms.

"Noodles! God, I'm glad to see you. The

whole time you were inside I . . ." Fat Moe blubbered some more words that Noodles couldn't decipher over the noise of the jazz band, which had struck up another raucous tune.

Releasing himself from Moe's clutch, Noodles said to the three of them, "You bunch of shtunks, you couldn't come and get me."

Cockeye pointed to Max. "He's the shtunk."

"He said you weren't getting out till Monday," Patsy added.

Laughing, Max said, "You can go next time he gets out."

Noodles waved at Max, giving him the finger, the universal up-yours.

Just then a redheaded fatty glued her mouth to Noodles, sucking his breath away. When she finally let him up for air, she said, "Let's see if you can guess who it is."

Snapping his fingers, Noodles replied, "Charlotte russe with whipped cream."

"You got it, kid," Peggy howled, her face still beautiful despite the fact that she now weighed well over two hundred pounds.

Looking her over, Noodles added, "A lot of it, too!"

"I still love 'em. As if you couldn't tell. But my price has gone up. I work in a high-class joint and get paid by the pound."

Opening his arms to embrace her, Patsy said, "And Peg's worth every penny, my red-hot mama!" Grabbing her around the waist, he attempted to lift her; when she didn't budge, he gave a wink and pretended to pass out from the exertion.

They all laughed, and Max said, "Okay, you've seen your old pals, now come meet some new ones." He started to move through the crowd, beckoning them to follow.

The others started after him, but Fat Moe grabbed Noodles' arm and pointed out a girl with white skin, blue eyes, and jet-black hair. "Remember her?" he asked.

Coolly she walked across the room to him and Noodles realized that his knees were shaking. "Aren't you going to say hello?"

"Deborah?"

She nodded. Across the room the others had stopped talking and were watching them. Max, annoyed, went to the bar. Fat Moe, like a puppy, stood beaming at them. Noodles and Deborah didn't speak, just looked at each other, neither knowing what to say. Deborah was happy to be admired and Noodles was happy to do the admiring. Finally his gaze began to make her uncomfortable, and her look of slight disdain was replaced with one of hunger and yearning.

There was noise all around them, but you could hear their silence.

At last Noodles spoke. "Your brother's a real buddy."

"He's romantic."

"Max tell you I was getting out today?"

"Max? No."

Looking hopeful, Noodles asked, "You remembered yourself?"

She let him hope for a moment before she said, "Moe told me. It's always Moe."

Hiding his disappointment, Noodles joked, "You mean you weren't counting the days?"

"Of course I was. Four thousand two hundred and nineteen, four thousand two hundred and eighteen . . . I lost count somewhere around three thousand."

"Yeah. And you didn't take time off for good behavior."

"Was your behavior good?"

"Look, it wasn't my choice."

"Yes, it was, Noodles. It's always your choice. You can't blame it on anyone else." She glanced across the room to where Max, obviously impatient, was signaling to Noodles. "It still is."

Noodles followed her eyes, saw Max. "Anyway, you came to welcome me back."

"I still live here. I was getting ready to go

out, and Moe said I should at least come and say hello."

"Did he have to bend your arm?"

"No, I wanted to come. Welcome back, Noodles. I hope it wasn't too awful."

"It was a long time. You think about people . . . a person."

"You can't do that. You have to keep busy, get on with your life. You can't live in the past . . . or the future."

From across the room, they heard Max's voice. "Noodles!"

Ignoring him, Noodles asked, "Dance? You still dancing?"

Smiling that secret smile he remembered from when he used to spy on her, she answered, "Of course. Every night. On the stage. I'm in a show at the Palace, and right now I'm late. I kept busy, Noodles, and I've made some progress since I danced here with the mops and the empties. You can come some night, if you have the time, and spy on me again."

He laughed. "Every night. Front row center. No, in a box, where it'll be dark and you won't know I'm there."

"I'll know. I always knew."

"Noodles!" Max's tone was quarrelsome now; his was a voice used to being obeyed.

"Go on, run. Your mother's calling you."
Then her voice softened and she added, "So long, Noodles. It's good to see you again."

"My pleasure."

"I worried . . ." But she didn't finish; instead she turned and ran through the crowd.

Noodles followed her with his eyes, then joined Patsy, Cockeye, and a pissed-off Max through a door marked PRIVATE.

The office looked brand-new. To Noodles, after a long stretch up the river, it looked like somthing from a movie, with its gleaming athletic equipment, highly polished furniture, and green-felt-covered billiard table. Near the table was a rack for the cues, and Max headed straight for it. Touching the cue rack in a certain spot, Max opened a hidden door to the delicatessen and restaurant, where Fat Moe waited with an empty tray.

Nodding toward the deli, Max asked quietly, "You got the wine?"

"Dago red—the best."

Moe stepped aside to let Max and the others pass. The room they entered was dimly lighted. A little illumination filtered in from the street lamps outside. The four friends walked toward a table where three people were sitting, mugs of beer in front of them.

The three men nodded, as if to say that the four young men were free to pass this particular frontier.

An elegant man, small-boned and equally small in stature, with the confident air of someone used to giving orders, was sitting at a corner table near the stove. Another man, coarser, was busy shoveling food in his mouth.

The elegant man spoke. "Well, they're all here. The four horsemen of the Apocalypse. Did you see that movie, Joe?" Joe was too busy eating to care. He grunted in the negative.

The slim man looked Noodles over with a mixture of curiosity and affection. "So this is the famous Noodles."

Max answered for Noodles, who didn't know what to say. "This is Mr. Frankie, Noodles."

The small man grew effusive. "Frankie. Call me Frankie. People I respect can call me Frankie. Man serves his time and stays quiet, him I can respect. Get yourselves some chairs and glasses, boys."

As Patsy and Cockeye brought up chairs and glasses, Frankie continued, "Welcome home, son. Sit down." With a courtly gesture he indicated the heavyset man who was still gobbling down food. "Boys, this is Joe.

He's come alla way from Detroit to ask me a favor. And I'm gonna do it. You know who Joe is. I don't need to tell you how far he's got or how far he's gonna get. He's not just a friend. He's a brother."

Joe grunted. "Only a Jew could eat this shit. Even mustard doesn't help." He looked up from his plate and eyed the boys while he continued to chew. Swallowing finally, he asked, "They in the family, Frankie?"

Frankie smiled, his eyes looking into the eyes of each of the young men in turn. He turned to Joe and said, "Not yet. But they're as good as in the family. After this week they'll have made their mark, Joe. Now tell the boys what they have to do. Listen to Joe. Joe's family."

Joe said, "I'm interested in some diamonds. Kid stuff."

The others looked at Noodles as if they expected him to speak for them. Finding his voice for the first time since they had entered the deli, he asked, "Why us?"

"Why not you?" Joe asked, still chewing.

Noodles nodded toward the three men seated at the table near the center of the room. "Don't the kids from Detroit feel like playing?"

Frankie held his hand up. "For right now,

Noodles, Joe needs it handled from the outside. His people are—what do I wanna say?—well-known in Detroit. Outside help that no one recognizes is needed. And the diamonds can't wait. Joe heard they're leaving for Holland soon. Don't worry." He smiled. "There's insurance. Joe, tell the boys about the prick insurance."

His mouth was still full and his lips were greasy, but Joe smiled, too. He reached into his vest pocket, brought out a toothpick, and began to clean his teeth as he spoke, his voice for the first time suggesting something near to relish.

"Ah! Life is just one big coincidence. The jeweler's secretary, she's this mousy blonde, I never paid much attention to her. She's the wife of my insurance agent, only I did notice that for a mousy dame she's got a great ass. Well, this agent, he sold me policies on everything you can think of: life insurance, fire insurance, disaster insurance, the works. I'm makin' him a rich man. One night I says to him, 'Edward, would you insure my cock for me? That's the one thing I care about most in the world. The day I can't get it up, you gotta pay off.' You know, he took me serious. Maybe he figures to make an extra buck. 'It can be done,' he says. 'But when we sign the policy, we gotta be sure the thing works.' I tell him, 'You leave me alone with your wife and she can tell you if it works or not.' I'm only joking but he doesn't say no, and so I'm lucky twice, 'cause the dame fucks like a bunny and then she talks. She fucks and then she tells me everything about her job. Where they keep the diamonds, who's in the office, everything you'd wanna know if you was gonna heist the place."

"I guess she's lookin' forward to it, boys." Frankie grinned.

Joe smiled as he recalled the experience. "Treat her gentle—if you can."

CHAPTER 11

From the outside it was just another office door. Inside, though, the Van Linden premises looked like a miniature version of the most secure portion of a bank. Metal cabinets and a large safe were in a small room that could be reached only by going through a cagelike wire door. The outer room, filled with typical desks and office furniture, was outfitted with alarm buttons. The shades on the one window were perpetually drawn. As a final touch, the door that led to the hall had a spy hole so that, when the doorbell rang, anyone inside could check out the visitor without being seen.

Carol, the secretary, went to the spy hole to answer the ring. She peeked out and saw the large nose, horn-rimmed glasses, and red hair of a face she saw every day, all day long, her boss. Smiling, she pushed the button and the automatic lock clicked the door open, but she jumped back as Van Linden was shoved into the room by four masked men carrying guns. Carol looked terrified but didn't utter a sound. One of the men closed the door. The two clerks in the office reacted immediately. The first one dived for an alarm bell, but before he could reach it, he was knocked unconscious to the floor by the butt of a gun. The second man started toward the window, but he, too, was tripped up, slashed across the face with the barrel of a pistol before joining his colleague on the floor.

The girl was taking it all in, her expression one of rapt fascination, as though she were turned on by the violence, the faceless monsters, and their large weapons. As the two clerks slumped to the floor, she breathed a low-pitched scream that was more a sound of lust than fear.

Quickly Cockeye and Patsy tied up the employees and cut the telephone wires. Noodles kept his eye on the girl, noticing how her eyes caressed his gun, while Max shoved the owner of the establishment, Van Linden, into the wire cage that housed the safe.

"Open it," Max said.

When Van Linden, despite his fear, shook his head and answered, "No," Max lashed out with his fist, smashing the old man in the jaw, sending his red wig and yarmulke flying across the room as blood spurted from his nose and mouth.

The girl threw herself toward Max, screaming, "You animals! Bastards!"

Noodles grabbed her and held her tight. As she tried to claw her way loose, he whispered, "Can it," covering her mouth with his free hand.

The old man was blubbering in fear and pain as Max towered over him, quietly repeating the words, "Open it."

"Please . . ." Van Linden's plea was cut off as once again Max's fist made contact with his tearstained face.

Wiggling free of Noodles, Carol bit the hand covering her mouth. When Noodles jumped back, she screamed at Max, "You rotten sons of bitches."

Noodles got hold of her again and she whispered into his ear, "Hit me, too! Hit me!" She was practically begging for it.

"What for? Cut the goddamn act. You'll get hurt."

Her voice was frantic. "Please! Hit me, go on, hit me. I love it. Please!"

Cockeye, finished trussing up the clerk, turned to Noodles and said, "Go on, hit her. She said 'please.' "

Carol began to squirm, trying to free herself from Noodles. He looked into her face and without warning gave her a good right hand on the side of the head, driving her back toward the room with the safe. She continued to scream, more in pleasure than in pain. By the safe, her boss had finally realized what his options were and had taken the key from his pocket and was attempting to turn it and at the same time work the combination on the safe, his fumbled movements like those of a drunk.

Max looked at Carol, then at Noodles. "She's gettin' on my nerves. Put a cork in her."

Noodles bashed her again, and when she fell to the floor, her skirt came up around her waist, exposing the fact that she was wearing no underwear. Noodles pulled her toward a corner, out of the way, and while she kept up her insults and screaming, threw himself on her body. Her resistance to his sexual attack was only technical; he was giving her exactly what she craved.

"Bastards," she continued to scream. "Shits!"

Finally, the old jeweler got the safe open. Max stepped forward and tapped him on the head with the butt of his gun. "Thanks," Max said. He called to Patsy and Cockeye, "Okay, boys, let's get to work."

They did just that, rifling through the safe, tossing papers and ledgers onto the floor until they came to the bottom, which turned out to be, as they had been told, false. When they removed it, they found a small chamois sack. In it were forty or fifty diamonds.

After checking the contents of the bag, Max said, "Let's go."

He paused at the office door and smiled at Noodles, who was adjusting his pants.

Cockeye called to Noodles, "We're finished with our business. How much longer for yours? We gotta tie her up."

"I'm done, too."

Cockeye grabbed some rope and quickly tied Carol's hands and feet. As they went out the door, Max said to Noodles, "One day out of jail and already you're Public Fucker Number One."

Laughing, the four men left the office, took off the handkerchiefs that had covered their faces, and stepped into the elevator, looking like four young businessmen, which, of course, they were.

It was an isolated country road, one where no cars were likely to appear and where pedestrians were nonexistent. Set off from the road, a few hundred feet away, was a low building, a factory of some sort, overlooking a small lake. Except for a low hum coming from the one building in the area, everything was quiet.

Cockeye, at the wheel, drove slowly down the road. When he spotted the limo, he kept on driving until he was fifty or so yards beyond it; then he made a careful U-turn and drove to within thirty feet, where he pulled the car off the road and stopped, but left the motor idling.

"That was Joe," Max said, "in the back seat. His boys are with him."

"Reasonable," Noodles answered.

"Maybe. But if we wanted to rip him off, we'd have just kept on goin' from the jewelers."

"You think he's got something planned?" Noodles asked. "A surprise party?"

"Could be."

"No, he knows Frankie'd be pissed. It's a straight business deal, Max. We deliver the goods, he pays the money."

Max didn't answer. Instead, he handed the chamois bag to Patsy. "Take it up to him. You know what to do."

Patsy nodded, climbed out of the car, and sauntered over to the limousine. Joe and one of his thugs sat in the back seat, the two others in the front.

Patsy tapped on the rear window. The thug rolled it down and Joe looked up at Patsy. "Well?"

Patsy leaned in and deposited the bag of diamonds in Joe's lap. Carefully Joe reached into his pocket and took out a jeweler's loupe, screwed it in under the thick brow of his right eye, and like an expert, carefully inspected the contents of the bag. He grunted one or twice, and then put the diamonds back into the bag, which he placed on his lap. With the loupe still covering one eye, he said, "Pay the kid." One of the men passed Patsy a roll of bills.

Patsy smiled, tucked the bills into his pocket, and straightened up as Joe asked, "Any trouble?"

"Kid stuff."

Still looking through the louper, Joe couldn't believe what he was seeing as the enlarged and deformed nose of a pistol appeared in Patsy's hand. Before he could react, it went off and drove the lens of the loupe straight into his head. Joe fell, scattering the diamonds onto the car floor. Before the sound of the shot had died away, Patsy turned his gun on the driver, pulled the trigger, and shot the man through the nape.

At the same time, Cockeye gunned the motor of their car and drove past the sitting-duck limousine. Max grabbed the Thompson submachine gun from the seat beside him, spraying the car and taking out the second of Joe's men. The third thug somehow managed to leap out of the other side.

Totally taken aback by what had happened, Noodles sat still until he saw the surviving Detroit man leave the car. His reflexes working, he yelled a warning to Cockeye, "Turn around!" Rubber squealed as Cockeye jammed on the brakes and pulled the car around. Gun in hand, Noodles jumped out before the car had come to a halt and followed the man into the red-brick factory building.

Noodles burst into the workroom, his gun waving. A couple of workers with linen masks covering their faces were already taking cover behind a huge machine covered by wire mesh. A cloud of feathers as white as snow tumbled from the mouth of the machine.

Looking around, Noodles noticed one of

the men staring in the direction of an L-shaped wing of the building. He eased himself up to the entrance and peered around the corner in time to see a shadow flatten itself against a wall behind another machine that was evidently not in use. As Noodles looked out, a shot whined through the air and a slug hit harmlessly, burrowing into the wall a few feet from where he was standing.

Beside his head Noodles noticed a control panel that was connected to the silent machine by a string of wires. Reaching up, he threw the switch. A Niagara of feathers poured out of the machine, engulfing the thug in his hiding place behind it. Covered with them, he staggered forward, still shooting, but blindly. He groped his way toward Noodles, who fired point-blank into the man's chest, so that the white feathers dripped red as the man sank to the floor. Noodles reached up, turned off the machine, and then went back through the factory, oblivious of the terrified workers who cowered as he went by.

Outside, Noodles headed for the car. He was stunned by what Max had ordered, by what he had done himself. And he was furious for not having been told what was going to happen. The car, its motor still running, was waiting for him, the others inside. Noodles yanked open the door on the driver's side and spoke to Cockeye.

"Get in back."

Cockeye climbed out, crawling into the back of the car while Noodles jumped in behind the wheel, put the car in gear, and pulled away so fast that Cockeye was almost thrown out.

"Hey, take it easy, Noodles," Cockeye called out. "You wanna leave me behind?"

His face drawn and tense, Noodles didn't answer. Max, sitting in the seat beside him, watched in silence.

"Why didn't you tell me?" Noodles said to Max.

Max thought a moment before he answered. "Being inside can change you. I'd already made a deal with Frankie to get rid of Joe, and with Frankie you don't say yes and then say no. I couldn't take a chance you'd say no. Besides, for all we know, they were ready to do the same thing to us."

"You were right. I woulda said no. A great big no."

"Then you wouldn't have been using your head. Frankie's as big as they come. He's got the Combination in the palm of his hand."

"Yeah. And he'll have us in his hands if we let him."

"You don't get nowhere alone. *You* oughta know that."

"Aren't you the guy that said he didn't like bosses? It sounded to me like a good idea then. And it still does."

Again Max was silent for a moment. Finally he said, "Let's think about it, Noodles. They're gonna ask us to come in with them. There's a lot in it for us. Think about it."

They'd come to a small wooden bridge and Noodles slammed on the brakes. "I am thinking about it. Today they asked you to get rid of Joe. Tomorrow they can ask me to get rid of you. Maybe that's okay for you, but not for me. I wanta remember who my friends are—and I don't wanta have to be worried maybe they forgot who *theirs* are."

Max smiled. "All right. You win. Let's forget it. For now." He looked out at the waters of the lake. "Let's go for a swim."

Noodles grinned. "Okay. Good idea." With that he gunned the motor and turned the car onto the bridge so that its running board snapped the railing off like bowling pins. Suddenly, he jerked the wheel and the car plunged a few feet down into the lake. Moments later Patsy and Cockeye, spitting water, emerged from just above where the car had sunk. Then Max came up, but there was no sign of Noodles.

Nearby, on the bank, a huge steam shovel was dredging dirt from the lake bottom. It lifted its dripping jaws from the water, swiveled, and puked its load out into a truck before turning back to scoop again.

12

1968

On the television set stuck up in the corner of Fat Moe's luncheonette, the black-and-white picture of the city's latest disaster, an explosion that had destroyed a shiny black limousine, was accompanied by the dulcet tones of the station's anchorman.

"District Attorney James Lister was killed in the explosion of a car belonging to State Secretary of Commerce Christopher Bailey as he, Lister, was leaving the secretary's Long Island estate.

"Lister was to testify Thursday before the

Senate committee investigating what has come to be called the Bailey Scandal.

"Secretary Bailey could not be reached for comment at this time, but we do have a statement from his legal adviser, Irving Gold."

Noodles was the only customer in the place who was paying any attention to what was being shown on the picture tube. Fat Moe kept looking over at him as he served his customer.

The television image changed and a sharply dressed, middle-aged man with slicked-down hair appeared on the screen. Superimposed on the picture was his name:

IRVING P. GOLD

A disembodied voice addressed the blank-faced lawyer. "Mister Gold, District Attorney Lister is the second witness in the Bailey Scandal to meet a sudden and violent end. As you know, the first was Thomas Finney, Under Secretary of Commerce, who fell to his death from his fifteenth-floor office only a month ago." There was a quick cut-in of a crumpled body lying on a sidewalk.

The voice went on. "Do you feel there's a connection between these two deaths?"

The raspy voice of Irving Gold answered smoothly, "The FBI is looking into it. Ask them."

Fat Moe sidled over to where Noodles sat. "Do you know those guys?" When Noodles shook his head, Moe said to him, "Take the money and run, Noodles. What the hell's keeping you here?"

"Curiosity."

The camera came back to the wooden-faced lawyer. Again the invisible questioner spoke. "The only remaining witness is the man who, rightly or wrongly, has given his name to this whole affair. I'm referring to Secretary Christopher Bailey, your client. What does the secretary think of all this?"

The image on the screen replied, "The secretary has no worries."

"If he has no worries, why has he retreated to his place on Long Island? Why has he refused interviews? Why doesn't he come to his office?"

Patiently, as though talking to a child, Gold answered, "Far from retreating, he's busy preparing his attack on the questions he will be asked next week by the committee."

"I'd call them accusations more than questions."

"False accusations."

"But accusations that must be answered."

"I repeat, the secretary has no worries."

"But the public does. There have been rumors of rigged contracts, bribery, the international Mafia, and especially the illegal use of the transport union's pension funds. Can you tell us anything about that?"

The picture on the screen switched to the exterior of an imposing building. A close-up revealed the words, TRANSPORT UNION. Then there was a wider shot and an elderly man, white-haired, limping, and carrying a cane, started walking toward the camera with a newsman who was holding a microphone. The white-haired man spoke.

"I deny all these rumors and accusations directed at my organization. It's just another typical example of trying to bust a union that has fought hard to protect the rights of the workingman."

When the man got closer to the screen, Noodles' interest intensified. Trying to place the man, he searched back through his memory. It wouldn't come until, when the man's face loomed large, another superimposed caption identified the speaker as JIMMY CONWAY, PRESIDENT, TRANSPORT UNION.

"Ah," Noodles said to Fat Moe. "This one I know."

The voice on the screen continued in a lilting accent. "All my life I've fought to keep my boys clean and clear of underworld contacts and dirty politics."

Noodles said to no one in particular, "He's

still handing out the same old crap." He looked back at the screen in time to hear Conway say, "If mistakes have been made in this situation, don't look at us. . . ."

Noodles smiled. It was all coming back to him; his memory was clear now. So long ago and yet it seemed like yesterday. More than thirty years ago. They were all young then, and all alive . . . although that particular day Conway had almost died. That was back in the thirties when union chiefs weren't universally hailed as statesmen, when they were never invited to the White House. Yes, it was all clear, the image in his mind sharper than the one on the television screen. . . .

It was 1933, and Noodles and the others were watching from behind a truck parked near the abandoned ferryboat dock. By now they were used to violence, but what they were witnessing was making them sweat.

Bubbling like pink champagne, the gasoline in one of the two glass measuring tanks drained through the hose held in the huge paw of a cretin named Willie, who was nicknamed, for obvious reasons, the Ape. The Ape was pointing the nozzle into the face of a young man tied hand and foot and lying in a cement pit about three feet deep. Willie kept the gas pumping until he had drenched the man in the pit from head to foot.

Next to Willie stood an even more disgusting specimen of humanity, a long, bony man with a tiny head, the face of a cadaver, and the eyes of a cobra. Chicken Joe, as he was called, moved to a crate on the opposite side of the pit, sat down, reached into his pocket, and took out a box of matches. He removed one, struck it, and held it aloft over the gasoline-filled pit, flipping it away just as it burned out. Then he laughed.

The rotted planks and rust-bound iron pilings attested to the fact that this pier had been out of use for many years. The game that was being played was likely to go on uninterrupted for as long as the sadistic hoods chose to torment their captive.

Off in the distance lights from the city blinked like signals for help, signals that would never be answered. Chicken Joe took a cigarette from a pack, struck another match, and paused before lighting the cigarette to ask a question.

"What's this I read about in the paper, Conway?" He applied the match, dragged on the cigarette, and coolly blew out the match before continuing. " 'Union chief burns management with accusations . . .' " He spun the spent match into the pit. It landed on the young man's shoulder and, still smoking, rolled to the ground.

Lighting another match, Chicken Joe again quoted aloud, " 'Fiery speech on the radio ...' " He blew out the match, tossed it toward the figure in the pit. Lighting still another, he held it aloft like a torch, saying, "What do you suppose they're gonna say tomorrow?"

From below the voice of young Jimmy Conway sounded hollow, but he managed to keep his cool under fire.

"Not a thing. Because in a little while you boys are gonna let me go. Sure now, your employer isn't daft enough to make a martyr of me. He wouldn't want folks to know the bosses hire thugs, hoodlums in the pay of politicians. It wouldn't be good for business, now, would it?"

For an answer Chicken Joe struck another match and said, "Union chief's flaming last words." He blew out the match and flipped it into the pit.

Conway raised his head. "Do it. Go ahead. You won't stop the workers or the social movement. People are sore, they're hungry, their kids have to eat."

Chicken Joe leaned forward, looking down into the hole. "Listen to me, you social shithead, we don't give a fuck about the workers and their movements. We just want you out of the factory so we can get working again." Reaching into his pocket, he pulled out a heavy envelope and waved it at Conway. "This is the last offer you're gonna get. You gonna sign it or not?"

"Tell your bosses they can wipe their asses with that."

Chicken Joe called over to Willie the Ape. "Douse him good. I only got one match left."

As Willie reached again for the pump, three sets of car headlights blazed on behind them, splitting the darkness. Momentarily blinded, Chicken Joe and Willie whirled around and then dived for cover in the pit, guns drawn, like soldiers in the trenches, peering over the edge.

What they saw was a man coming forward, alone, walking easily into the light. Portly and well-tailored, the man raised a pudgy hand and called out, "Hold it!"

Shielding his eyes with his hand, Chicken Joe called to the man, "Crowning?"

"That'll do, boys." His tone told everything—the boss had arrived.

Puzzled but reassured, the two men climbed out of the pit. "What'll do?" Chicken Joe called out. Then, lowering his voice, he added, "We nearly got the kid where we want him."

At that point Noodles, Patsy, Max, and Cockeye emerged from behind the truck, their machine guns aimed at the boss, the man called Crowning.

Max, in his usual calm, mocking voice, said, "And we got the boss right where we want him."

As the hands of the two thugs tightened around their guns, Cockeye intervened. "Easy! We're just swappin' prisoners. No one gets hurt."

"Union for management," Patsy added, giving Crowning a little push.

"Well, look who's here," Chicken Joe said. "Fat Moe's boneyard boys. Bury any good stiffs lately?"

"Which reminds me," Max said. "How's that cancer in your gut coming along, Chicken Joe?" Chicken Joe looked daggers at Max, who only laughed. "Untie him." Max nodded toward Jimmy Conway, who had been watching the scene with surprised attention but with no sign of relief and no apparent sympathy for the rescue squad.

Hysterically, Chicken Joe began to twitch, screaming, "I don't take orders from you!"

"We're not asking you to take orders," Noodles said. "We're telling you."

"Untie him," Crowning said.

Willie the Ape climbed quickly back into

the pit and loosened the bonds on Conway's hands and feet. When he was done, Cockeye reached down to give Conway a hand, but the union leader ignored him, instead jumping out on his own and immediately tearing off his sopping, gasoline-soaked outer garments. He eyed his rescuers with distaste.

"Who are you guys?" he asked. "Who's payin' you?"

"Don't get your Irish up," Cockeye said. "It was one of your boys."

"You go tell him I don't want you in with us. Our fight's got nothin' to do with booze and dope and babes." He looked over at Crowning, adding scornfully, "That's their way, not ours. Mother of God, there's gotta be some some difference between us."

Noodles took off his overcoat and tossed it to the angry young man, saying, "There's a difference, all right. They'll win, like always, and you and your men'll get it up the ass, like always."

Crowning nodded, giggling. "Sooner than you think."

Standing outside police headquarters, poised on the granite steps like a Roman conqueror, stood Police Chief Aiello. A heavyset man in a crisp blue uniform holding a bunch of flowers, he posed for the photographers, who popped magnesium flashguns over the shoulders of the waiting reporters.

He started slowly down the steps as they peppered him with questions.

"Chief Aiello, moving policemen into the factory surprised everyone—the press, the unions, especially the strikers. And the public."

"What do you want, sweetheart, a declaration of war? Surprise gives you an advantage. Besides, ours was a peaceable operation."

Another reporter, this one a man, asked, "But wasn't it contrary to the new union laws—and the rights of the strikers?"

"Sonny, I'm chief of police, not chief of the people. My job is to keep the peace, see the laws are obeyed, and protect property."

"Was there violence on the part of the strikers to justify your action?"

"There could have been. What I say is 'Prevention, not repression.' "

"But you let the scabs take over and start working." It was the woman reporter who spoke again.

"Call them unemployed workers if you want to talk to me, little lady." By now the chief had arrived at his car. He stopped and added, in a wholly different tone, "Now, with your permission, I want to take these flowers to my wife before they wilt." Giving a proud wink, he added, "Maybe you've heard I'm the father of a baby boy."

Another reporter shouted out, "We've heard he's the youngest stockholder in that factory you occupied."

Aiello's face turned bright red. Angrily he asked, "Just what do you mean by that, young fella?"

"They say the management expressed their thanks with a little birthday present to the baby."

Grabbing the reporter by the collar, Aiello yelled in his ear, "Slander's a serious offense—especially from a second-string reporter. You wanna find out how serious?" Suddenly he relaxed his grip and smiled, letting the reporter go. "But seeing this is my first boy after four girls ... I declare amnesty. Behave yourselves."

He got into the car, slammed the door behind him, and said to the driver, "The hospital."

At the same time that the chief was holding court on the steps of the police station, four young men, dressed in white smocks and face masks, were entering the hospital nursery.

The maternity ward was a large, rectangular room surrounded by soundproof glass walls that separated the room from the corridor. There were some thirty wicker cribs containing babies, most of them wailing, lining the glass walls so the children could be seen but not heard by visitors. A curtained doorway led into the room, and a nurse, carrying a newborn infant in each arm, disappeared out the side door toward the dispensary.

As the nurse left, the four men, all brisk and businesslike, bustled into the nursery through the opposite door. Three of them went directly inside, while the fourth stationed himself at the curtain as a kind of guard.

Noodles grabbed an infant from a nearby crib and changed him with one in the second row. Then he turned to Patsy, who held pencil and paper poised. "Fourteen to twenty-six; twenty-six to fourteen." After getting that down, Patsy turned to Max, who was also switching babies.

Max said, "Eighteen to thirty-two; thirty-two to seven. Seven goes to eighteen. Don't screw it up."

"You kiddin'? I got a memory like a blind bookie."

The operation continued as the three men busied themselves with creating confusion. The tempo of their work grew faster as the wails of the babies grew louder. From the curtained door Cockeye peeked in, watching the frenzied work of his friends, his wide grin hidden behind his mask.

Hearing the sound of footsteps behind him, Cockeye turned in time to see a young nurse, her name card pinned to the blouse of her uniform, bearing down on him. Blocking the doorway, he lowered his mask and assumed an air of stern severity.

Before she could question his presence, he asked, "Miss Thompson, why weren't you on hand to meet us? Didn't the office tell you we were coming?"

Caught off guard, the woman could only shake her head in the negative.

Before she could say anything, he went on. "You've heard of me, Doctor Karlsberg, ears, eyes, nose, and throat. I'm in town with Doctors Schumann, Carlucci, and Freiberg for the pediatrician's convention sponsored by the Carnegie Foundation. Didn't I see you there?" His machine-gun-like delivery kept the girl dumbfounded. Now he changed his tactics, fixing her with a lust-laden eye. "What are we doing tonight?"

Ignoring him, she tried to get by. "Excuse me, Doctor, but it's breast-feeding time."

"All right, but remember, it was your idea."

"Doctor Karlsberg!"

"Call me Alfred," he said.

Before she could say more, the three other men hurried out through the curtained doorway, their masks up to disguise their features. Nodding curtly to the nurse, Cockeye scurried after them, leaving behind a desperate wailing of babies.

CHAPTER
13

The private hospital room was filled to capacity. Flowers; four little girls; the broad expanse of Mrs. Aiello, sitting up in bed, buxom and beaming like a fecund queen; and her equally large and beaming husband—the Aiello clan seemed to overpower the room so that, although it wasn't so, a passerby looking in would get the feeling there was not one inch of space left.

Sitting in a patriarchal position, Chief Aiello, who considered himself a benefactor of mankind, asked, "He's eating?"

Smiling indulgently, an old hand at the baby-feeding business, as her breasts would attest, Mrs. Aiello replied, "For five." Which, of course, was the exact number of their offspring.

Her husband reached over and patted the font from which the nourishment flowed. "Lucky for us we got our own dairy right here. Don't you feed him at four o'clock?"

"That's right. And here he is." A nurse appeared with the heir to the throne in her arms.

Aiello stood up and took charge of the baby. "Holy Mary, they change so fast." He stared into the baby's face. Smiling, he said, "Just like the old man. Same fire, same devilish eyes." Turning to his wife, he asked, "Did you get a good look at his pisello?"

Pleasantly scandalized, she responded, "Vincent! The girls!"

Aiello turned to the four little girls, who sat silent and fearful, huddled together on and around a chair. "You girls might as well know it now. After me, this is the boss in our house." Looking at the baby, his tone softened. "This kid's got balls, just like his papa." At that point he noticed that his sleeve was wet. He held the baby away from him and a look of slight distaste crossed his face.

The nurse was already prepared with a diaper. "Let me have him," she said.

"No, I'll do it. I want to look at his . . . at him."

He put the baby on the bed, unhooked the pins, and dropped the diaper flap. He stared hard for a second, looked again, then pushed the baby away.

"What the fuck is this?"

The nurse turned pale, checked the baby's tag, then her clipboard. "But that's the right number."

Aiello, his voice rising faster than a sky-rocket, screamed, "I'll break your neck! You find my son or I'll burn down the whole goddamn hospital."

Just then the telephone rang. Dashing for it, Aiello was screaming "Hello!" before he even picked up the receiver. "Hello!" His face turned pale and he began to sweat profusely. "Who the hell are you? What? Where is he?"

Mrs. Aiello began to sob.

Noodles, looking very snazzy in his tuxedo, sat at the telephone. Sprawled around on sofas and armchairs were Max, Patsy, and Cockeye, drinks in hand. During the day the office of Peggy's brothel had a sedate if some-what overdecorated look. Noodles grinned at his friends and raised his voice so they could hear the conversation he was having with the totally confused chief of police.

"Where do you think he is? In the maternity ward. Never left. Only he had a little bed rash and we had to change his cradle." He held the phone away from his ear as Aiello screamed curses at him.

Peggy, ample and flashy, sat nearby at her desk, going over her accounts. From time to time she looked up at the boys and winked.

"Relax, Chief. You don't want to have a heart attack, do you? You'd never see your little kid grow up if you did. . . . No! No! I told you everything is all right. Thank God we were there to keep an eye on things. We can put all the little tikes right back where they were, if we feel like it. You get that? *If* we feel like it. Right now, we do. But you gotta meet us halfway. . . . What the hell have you got to do with the strike? Get your men outta there and let the strikers make their own deal with the bosses, you get me? Then we'll give you Junior's number . . . that's the ticket. You're a rotten son of a bitch, Aiello, but you're not an actual prick, and we'd like to help you out. I'll call you back."

Noodles put down the receiver and turned to the others. "Great guy. Real conversationalist." To Patsy he said, "Where's the list?"

Looking slightly embarrassed, Patsy began

to finger through his pockets. "Let me think . . ."

The others watched him in silence as he got up and looked through his pockets. Finally he owned up. "Seems to me I left it in that jacket at the hospital." His eyes lit up. "But I'm positive that the males were even numbers and the females were odd numbers."

Cockeye said, "What more do we need? At least he'll get a kid with a pecker."

Noodles shrugged. "So we give him an even number. Eight. If he's lucky, it might even be the right one."

Looking worried, Patsy asked, "And the rest of them?"

Cockeye jumped up. "Jesus, what if I got switched in the cradle!"

Max spread out his arms as if he were giving absolution. "We hand out destiny like animal crackers. Some get it good, and some get it right up the gigi."

Hauling herself up from her desk, her accounts in one hand and a roll of bills in the other, Peggy came to the center of the room. "It's Saturday, boys. Time to settle up."

Cockeye stood up and went over to a rather graphic picture of nymphs and satyrs hanging on the wall. He moved the picture aside, peered through a peephole, and called out, "I'll take mine in trade. Look at those luscious numbers, will ya? Stuff like that could keep you up forever."

In the office Noodles looked at the roll of bills. "This is too much, Peggy," he said.

"You want business should be worse?"

Patsy, speaking for them all, said, "Peggy, we talked it over . . ."

Noodles, bouncing the roll of bills in his hand, continued, "No more splitting the profits. We'll call this the first loan payment. The place is yours."

From his place at the wall, Cockeye called out, "Hey, look who's here. Come here, you guys."

Max got up and ambled over to Cockeye, saying to Peggy on the way, "That suit you, Peg?"

Although she was grateful, Peggy was no dummy. "No, thanks, boychiks, it don't suit me. Everything is smooth and quiet around this place because everyone knows you and me are partners. No cops, no city hall, no investigations . . ."

Max had replaced Cockeye at the wall. He looked through the peephole and called out, "Noodles. An old pal." When Noodles looked through to the other room, Max added, "The one by the victrola."

Noodles recognized the woman, but he couldn't quite place her. "Who's that?"

"What d'ya mean?" Max pretended to be scandalized. "You were going to marry her."

Cockeye, giving an impersonation, moaned and bit his lip. "Hit me. Beat me. You animal. I love it."

Noodles smashed his fist against his forehead. "Holy shit," he swore. "The Detroit cock-squasher."

Patsy made a dash for the peephole as Max said to Peggy, "Peggy, call in the redhead in the flowery dress, will you?" When Peggy went to the door, he added, "Tell her there's a bunch of fans out here."

Peggy called through the door, "Carol, would you come in here a minute?" When the girl appeared in the doorway, Peggy motioned to the boys and asked, "Friends of yours?"

"I don't think so. I'd remember a bunch of good-lookers like these." She smiled at the four men. Max took out his handkerchief and tied it over his face. The others followed suit and Carol beamed. "Of course, how could I forget?" she exclaimed. Then, with a touch of artless malice, she added, "Actually I was only acquainted with one of you personally."

"Which one?" Max asked, unbuttoning his fly. "Let's see how good a memory you got for faces." He removed his penis from his underwear and waved it at her. Taking their cue from him, the other three did the same, lining up for a modified short-arms inspection. Reviewing the troops, Carol finally pointed at Max.

"You!"

Max shook his head and pointed to Noodles. "Him."

When Carol looked embarrassed, Noodles said, "We're together so much we're startin' to look alike."

"Especially around the eyes," Max added.

Laughing, Carol pointed toward Noodles' cock. "So we've already met."

Skipping him, she moved down the line again, squeezing each of the men gently. "I'm Carol. Pleased to meet you. Hello there. Charmed. A real pleasure." She stopped at Max, lingering over him a bit longer than the others.

"The pleasure is all mine," Max said.

Pulling off his handkerchief, Carol brought her mouth to Max's for a long, lingering, sensual embrace.

Buttoning up, Patsy asked, "So you left Detroit?"

Answering for her, Peggy said, "No. Her and her husband just come in on weekends. She takes on ten guys with hubby watching through a peephole like that one."

"Well," Cockeye responded, "it sure beats the seashore. In fact, it beats the movies."

Removing her mouth from Max's, Carol pushed her hips seductively against his and began to sway in dancetime to the music that filtered in from the next room.

Patsy asked Noodles, "What do you think that schmuck is up to, in his cubbyhole right now?"

Noodles answered, "He must be asking himself, Where's my fuckin' wife?"

Dancing Max over to where Noodles was standing, Carol reached down and touched Noodles' crotch. "How about a threesome?"

Answering for Noodles, Max replied, "Look at the man in his monkey suit. Can't you see he's got other plans for tonight?"

Tauntingly Carol said, continuing to stroke Noodles, "Bring her along. We'll make it a foursome."

Roughly Noodles shoved her away. He went to an armchair and picked up his top-coat and a white silk scarf. Putting them on, he said to Carol, "You got the wrong guy. I'd belt you again, but you'd like it." Turning to the others, his face a mask of seriousness, he said, "Good night, boys. And girls. Don't wait up for me."

*　　*　　*

Times may have been bad for many Americans, but you wouldn't have known it from the glitter of Broadway, a street crowded with people, cars, and flashing neon signs. The theaters were jammed; marquees proclaimed that hit plays had been running for weeks, months, years, proving, if nothing else, that someone had money to spend.

It was eleven o'clock and curtains were down or going down on all of the hit shows. Chorus girls were exiting from the stage doors, meeting boyfriends or sugar daddies, while eager fans lined up to get a glimpse of a star, or perhaps, if lucky enough, an autograph. Noodles stood apart from the throng, his heart beating wildly. Deborah had been magnificent and now they were going to dinner.

Dressed in an evening gown with a fur wrap thrown casually around her shoulders, she came out the door. The crowds, overcome, parted for her and watched with admiration and envy as she moved straight to Noodles, who, with a courtly bow, offered her a bouquet of flowers.

"Been waiting long?" she asked.

"All my life." He put his arm carefully around her shoulder and steered her toward the car, winking at the chauffeur, who replied with an admiring grin.

CHAPTER
14

It was a restaurant by the sea, an elegant
one, far out on Long Island. Noodles led her
up onto the wide veranda and then inside,
where an attractive hatcheck girl took his
topcoat and her furs. A maître d' bustled
over and ushered them into the dining room,
acting as if he were escorting visiting royalty.
The band was playing a quiet little waltz,
the musicians all dressed in tuxedos, as were
the waiters who stood by in ranks waiting to
offer their services. A cigarette girl in a short
skirt and net stockings stood near the waiters.
Behind her were busboys, ready to bring
water, bread and butter, whatever was re-

quired by the affluent (for only the affluent could afford such a place) customers.

The tables were laid with silver and elegant china; a vase of freshly cut out-of-season flowers graced each one. A huge buffet, groaning with beef and lobster and a swan carved out of ice, was in the center of the room.

All the tables were laid out for two—and all of them were empty!

Deborah looked questioningly at Noodles while the smiling maître d' stood at attention nearby.

Noodles said, "You said you'd like a place by the sea. It's off-season and they're closed, but I had it opened. All tables for two. For you to choose."

Smiling and shaking her head in pleasurable disbelief, Deborah pointed to a table by a window where they could look out at the ocean. The maître d' led the way, seated Deborah, and signaled for the sommelier and the squad of waiters. Proffering the menu, he made several suggestions.

"We have boeuf à la mode. Or we have an exquisite blanquette de veau with a sauce—"

Deborah interrupted him. "I'll have the asperges, sauce vinaigrette, and then a Chateaubriand."

"Pommes frites?"

"Naturellement."

"Comme dessert? Torte de fraises ou—"

"I'll decide later."

The man turned his attention to Noodles. "And Monsieur?"

Reddening, Noodles answered abruptly, "The same."

"Ah! *La même chose. Certainement.*" He snapped his fingers and the waiters hustled off. Now the sommelier stepped forward wearing his *tâte-vin* as if it were the Hope diamond. Deborah put her gloves in her glass.

The wine steward turned to Noodles. "For the wine?"

"You order if you like," Deborah said. "I only drink water." With an awkward gesture, Noodles waved the man away.

"You decide, buddy," Noodles called after him. He was feeling uptight when he spoke to her. "Been around, haven't you? All the fancy dishes, parley-voo-fransay. Who's teaching you?" A note of jealousy crept into his voice.

She gave him a gentle smile and patted his hand. "A sugar daddy who teaches me how to behave in fancy restaurants, how to act in polite society? No. I read. I want to learn everything, Noodles. I want . . . I never want to go back to what I was. It's all part of my plans."

"It'd be nice," Noodles said, "if I were part of those plans."

"You're the only person that—"

"Say it."

"You're the only person I ever cared about. But . . ." Smiling at the intensity on his face, she tried to make a joke. "You'd lock me up and throw away the key, wouldn't you?"

Shrugging, Noodles laughed. "I guess so."

"What's worse is that I might even like it."

"So?"

"I wouldn't like it for long. I want to get where I'm going."

"Where's that?"

"Where everyone wants to get. To the top." She looked him in the eye and he stared back.

"You sound like Max. That's all he talks about. Making it big. Being the biggest. You're both alike. That's why you hate each other."

Angered slightly, she asked, "Do you want me to leave, Noodles?" Seeing she had hurt him, she softened, and the anger left as fast as it came. Smiling, she lapsed into a Jewish accent. "You dencing?"

Noodles looked surprised and then he remembered the old joke. "You esking?"

"I'm esking."

"I'm dencing."

Together they stood up and headed for their private dance floor. Noodles slipped his arm around her waist. A chorus line of waiters arrived bearing the meal, but Noodles and Deborah, locked in each other's arms like lovers, could not have cared less.

It was some time later. Stars twinkled in the sky, numberless; a silver sliver of moon could be seen hanging just over the horizon. The waves beat against the shore, marking time with the orchestra, which was playing somewhere beyond the dunes. The tune they played had been Noodles' request: "Amapola."

A wide Persian carpet was spread out on the sand; a soft breeze lifted the long aprons of the two waiters standing by with champagne and glasses. Deborah, stretched out on the carpet, had her face buried in the gardenias, listening to Noodles as he spoke. He was lying on his back, his hands behind his head, talking so quietly that his voice now and then would be lost in the murmur of waves and music.

"We'd go to bed when it was still day and they'd get us up when it was still night. And yet ... all those years in prison just seemed to fly by. Time passes a lot faster when you're not doing anything." He shifted his weight so that he could see the outline of her face.

"There were two things I used to dream about—the way Dominic said 'I slipped' just before he died—and you."

She didn't stir; he couldn't tell if she was awake, but there was something about the tilt of her head that made him believe she was catching every word.

"Do you remember how you read to me from the Song of Songs? I got in good with the chaplain because I was always borrowing his Bible. 'How beautiful are your feet in sand, O prince's daughter.' "

He reached out and gently caressed her leg. "I'd read it before I went to sleep, and I'd think of you. I remember another one. 'Your navel is a bowl well-rounded with no lack of wine, your belly a heap of wheat surrounded with lilies. Your breasts are clusters of grapes, your breath sweet-scented as apples . . .' "

Sitting up, he took her face in his hands with a tenderness that he didn't know he possessed, a tenderness that was infinite.

"No one's going to love you the way I loved you when I masturbated reading the

Bible. When I couldn't take prison anymore, I'd think, Deborah's out there, Deborah's alive, Deborah exists . . . and that'd get me through."

She lifted her hand to his, as if she meant to caress him. Then slowly she took his hands away from her face and looked full into his eyes.

"I'm leaving, Noodles. Tomorrow night. I'm going to Hollywood. I had to see you tonight to tell you."

Totally deflated, Noodles stared out the window from the back seat of the Rolls. The sky had clouded over, and all he could see were heavy black trees that seemed to swoop down like avenging angels at the car. Occasionally there would be a glare of oncoming headlights, illuminating the driver's head for a moment; then, like meteors in the sky, the lights would sweep by and he would be left again in blackness.

Deborah, as silent and thoughtful as he, sat beside him. Sensing his pain, she reached out, took his hand, and squeezed it gently. He returned the gesture, but with so much intensity that Deborah gasped with pain. He let go of her hand, and as he looked at her, she was struck by the despair she could see in his eyes. When he moved closer, she didn't shy away, but allowed him to take her in his arms, meeting his fierce embrace with a passion that matched his own. When finally she tried to pull back, Noodles refused to let her go, holding her tighter, his kisses more insistent than before. All the tenderness had gone out of him, replaced by the pent-up anger and violence that had been repressed for too long.

He began to kiss her neck and shoulders, forcing her fur wrap onto the floor. Trying to push him off but failing, she could see the other side of his nature, the fierce, pitiless, demanding Noodles, the slum kid gone from petty thief to remorseless killer, the man who knew only one way to get what he wanted: to take it and damned be anyone who stood in his way.

He tore at her clothing, ripping the silk dress and underthings away from her breasts, mauling them, scratching the sensitive skin on her neck and shoulders. He covered her mouth with his hand and forced his leg between her knees, pulling her back by the hair until she was beneath him on the seat. Then he was on top of her, entering her with quick, savage thrusts. When she was finally able to pull his hand away from her face, she uttered one loud, piercing scream.

The car slammed to a halt, jolting both of them forward onto the floor. The chauffeur opened the back door and stared down at them. "Are you trying to kill her?"

Stunned by his own violence and ashamed of what he had done, Noodles stumbled out of the car, adjusting his clothes, while the chauffeur helped the half-conscious Deborah, her clothing torn and bloody, back up onto the seat. All at once she threw the door open, fell from the car, and began to vomit hysterically into a ditch that paralleled the road. When she could retch no more, she stood up, arranged her torn dress as best she could, and wiped the blood from her thighs and body with her handkerchief.

Noodles looked away, unable to accept what he had done, unable to face her. Finally she got into the car and huddled in the corner of the back seat like a terrified animal.

Noodles handed the chauffeur a large bill. "Take her home," he said. "I'll walk."

The chauffeur took the money, looked at the denomination of the bill, then folded it up and tucked it in Noodles' breast pocket. He slid behind the wheel of the car and pulled away, leaving Noodles alone in the dark with a lifetime ahead of him in which he would never forget this night.

* * *

Two suitcases sat on the floor beside the restaurant table, a fur coat thrown over them. Deborah, looking pale but elegant, sat at the table alone. Finishing her coffee, she placed some money on the check that had been left by her saucer as a porter came by to pick up her luggage. She followed him across the almost empty dining room at the railroad station into the cavernous hall of the main room at Grand Central Station. They went toward the track where the Twentieth Century Limited, the train for Los Angeles via Chicago, was made up and boarding passengers preparatory to pulling out. The porter took her bags to the train platform and she started to look for the car that held her compartment.

Noodles, out of breath and unshaven, a raincoat and scarf thrown over his disheveled clothes, ran through the central part of the station, catching sight of her back as she started down the platform. He hurried after her.

By the time he got to the train, she was nowhere in sight. He ran from car to car, leaping up, looking in the windows, staring at the well-dressed people who still milled about on the platform. Finally he caught sight of her pale face through one of the windows.

She looked out and saw him staring at her. Their eyes met, and then very deliberately she lowered the shade, cutting him out of her life forever.

CHAPTER
15

Fat Moe's Speakeasy, like most bars and nightclubs, was dingy-looking in the daylight. Noodles, freshly showered, shaved, and looking like himself again in a clean, well-pressed suit, stepped out of the elevator into the empty, forlorn space that would in a few hours turn again into a magical spot where revelry and high times would help hide the realities of life from the participants.

The tinny sound of Cockeye's flute reached out from the inner office. A half-smile formed on his face. Cockeye and his flute. A reminder—and for Cockeye, an outlet. Noodles crossed the room to the half-opened door and entered the office.

He stopped short, staring at the sight that greeted him. A huge gilded chair, carved and embellished like a mogul's throne, sat on a raised platform on one side of the room. Sprawled on the throne, a fat cigar sticking out of his mouth, was Max. Sitting beside him on a chair so low that he might as well have been sitting on the floor was Cockeye, still playing his flute.

Patsy, a large bandage under his ear, stood beside Max; Carol was there, too, half-sitting, half-leaning on a corner of the pool table, aimlessly pushing the balls around on its felt surface. Near the other corner Fat Moe busied himself with a scrapbook and newspaper clippings that he had spread out on the desk and part of the pool table. When Noodles came in, Fat Moe looked up at him and then glanced nervously at Max.

Noodles took them all in with a brief glance, then focused his eyes and full attention on Max.

Max, taking the stogie from his mouth, spoke to Noodles. "Well, look who's back!"

Ignoring this sally, Noodles went to the chair and inspected the fancy carved scrollwork. "What's this?"

"It's a throne," Max answered proudly. "Belonged to the king of Romania. Eight hundred bucks."

From across the room, making her presence felt, Carol added, "It's from the sixteenth century."

Ignoring her, Noodles asked Max, "What are you doing with it?"

"I'm sittin' on it."

Suddenly he leapt up and went to the desk, opening the center drawer. He took out a roll of bills that he tossed at Noodles.

"The union paid off. That's your share." He hurried back to the throne as if afraid that in his absence it might be usurped. "While you were on vacation, we were working overtime."

Patsy pointed to his bandage. "Even Jimmy Clean-Hands respects us. Look at me. I shed blood for the cause of better wages, better working conditions, and solidarity forever, whatever the hell that means."

Fat Moe pointed to his clippings. "It's all in the papers." Noodles walked over to him and Moe added, "The *Daily Telegraph* didn't like it. It says here, 'Underworld Joins Strikers in Brutal Battle.' "

Noodles picked up the paper and read the headline:

GANSTERS CLASH AT FACTORY
OCCUPIED BY STRIKERS. TOTAL
LACK OF POLICE INTERVENTION

Fat Moe continued. "But the *Post* liked it. 'Ends Justify Means In Decisive Gangland Encounter.' And they're the ones who kvetched about the Atlantic City job."

Cockeye put down his flute long enough to say, "Reporters never know what the fuck they want."

Noodles weighed the roll of bills in his hand. "You could have looked for me."

"We did," Max told him. "Cockeye found you at the Chink's so doped up you didn't even recognize him."

Simpering, Cockeye added, "You called me Deborah."

Fat Moe, who had been taking it all in, suddenly got very interested in his clippings.

Taking a seat, his irritation showing, Noodles said, "It's my own fuckin' business what I do."

Max leapt up and crossed to him. "We do our fuckin' business together and fuckin' broads don't get in the way."

Noodles nodded toward Carol. "Then what's she doin' here? Couldn't she get enough in Detroit? They could screw her on the assembly line at the River Rouge plant, if they ever get it open."

Carol moved over to Max and said to Noodles, " 'Cause she's screwin' here. And only with him."

"With your husband watching through the keyhole?"

"I left him, wise guy, if it's any business of yours."

To Max, Noodles said, "So you two are living together and you bring her to work, and you tell me not to mix with broads."

Max screamed in Noodles' face. "You're forgetting one thing. I don't give a single, solitary shit about her."

Reacting as if she'd been hit, Carol cried, "Maxie!"

Sneering, Noodles asked, "Where do you two spend your weekends, at Peggy's cathouse?"

Ignoring the remark and pointing to Carol, Max asked, "You want me to dump her?" She tried to speak, but no words would come. Noodles just stared at Max. "You want me to kick her ass out of here?" He stared back at Noodles and repeated the question. "You want me to kick her in the ass?"

Noodles looked over at Carol and started to laugh, a long, loud, irrepressible laugh. Then, after a moment, Max laughed, too, joined by Patsy and Cockeye, even by Fat Moe, albeit a little nervously.

Carol grabbed her purse and gloves and slammed out of the room without a word.

Max and Noodles continued to laugh until the telephone rang.

Jimmy Conway stood in a telephone booth. He was in a small store in downtown Manhattan, empty except for one clerk. When the phone was picked up, he said, "It's Jimmy. Who's this? Max?"

From the receiver he heard a voice say, "No. Noodles."

"Okay, listen," Jimmy said. "We're going to need you guys today." He looked out through the storefront window to where a truck full of his friends, workers on strike, stood waiting. "I'm going to hit them with a tough speech and I think you guys—"

Suddenly Noodles heard the voice on the other end of the line stop, interrupted permanently by the shattering blast of a shotgun, then more gunfire, the sound of breaking glass, and finally, silence.

"Shit," he said over his shoulder to the others. "They shot him."

Then he heard the sound of yelling, screeching car tires, and a breathless voice said into the telephone, "It's Jimmy. He's in pretty bad shape. Two guys in a touring car. I recognized 'em from before. A big ape of a guy and a skinny one who looks like he's gonna croak . . ."

* * *

Crowning, as usual accompanied by his two minions, Chicken Joe and Willie the Ape, moved nervously along the sidewalk. There was to be a meeting soon, but in the meantime Crowning was apprehensive. You could never be too safe. He had learned that early in life when a good friend had been gunned down before his eyes. Looking around, he thought everything seemed fine, but he was worried all the same.

Their car was on the other side of the street, but crossing through the traffic was the least of his worries. He took a careful look in both directions, judged the coast to be clear, and nodded to Joe and Willie. The traffic was stopped at a light a block away and, except for two black men pushing a rack of cleaning toward the service entrance of a hotel, the street was momentarily empty.

The three men started across the street. They had not even reached the center line when they were cut down by a blast of machine-gun fire. Willie the Ape and Chicken Joe crumpled as Max and Noodles stepped out from the rack of clothes, each holding a smoking gun. A car pulled up, tires screeching, driven by Cockeye, and Patsy jumped out and covered the men behind the rack with two guns of his own. Noodles and Max scooted from their hiding place and jumped onto the running board of the car, followed by Patsy, as Cockeye took off. Crowning, unhit, stood frozen with fear as he backed away from the dead bodies of his two body-guards, moving back until he could go no farther, his back flat against the hotel wall. It was at that moment that he decided he had played the game long enough; it was time for him to get out while he still had his life.

The champagne cork popped, hitting the ceiling and bouncing down, striking the man lying in a cast in the hospital bed on the top of the head. Everyone laughed, including the immobile-from-the-waist-down patient, Jimmy Conway.

"Watch it!" someone called out, a phrase that was echoed as another cork popped.

Patsy turned to Conway and joked, "Flat-tened by a blast of Cordon Rouge. Machine-gun bullets couldn't get you in the head, but Cockeye pops you his first try."

Max, holding his overflowing glass aloft, said, "If the union boys could see you now, Jimmy, you'd never whip them into line."

The four boys, Conway, and a smooth-faced politician named Sharkey were crowded into Conway's room.

There was a strange note of bitterness in Conway's voice as he answered Max, "You're the ones with the whip."

"We won," Max said. "That's what counts. The *only* thing that counts."

Noodles handed Jimmy a glass of the bubbly. "It's tough not being there to sign the contract, huh, Jimmy?"

"What's tough is seeing you guys do in one day what I couldn't do in two years."

Sharkey spoke for the first time. "And you turned your nose up at them. You're lucky me and the boys in the party are lookin' out for the future of the union." Raising his glass for a toast, he said, "To the hottest newcomer in American labor—Jimmy Conway."

They all joined him. Conway stared down at his leg as the head nurse came in, followed by a couple of interns. She was breathing fire already over the unacceptable noise level, and when she saw the glass in Jimmy's hand, she lunged for it like a woman possessed, tearing it from his grasp and turning on the others. "You're nothing but criminals," she stormed.

"Does it show?" Cockeye asked sweetly.

Gesturing toward the interns, she continued, "We're about to take him to the operating room, and here you are giving him drinks."

The two interns started to push the bed, which was on wheels, through the door.

"Why operate," Conway protested, "if I'm going to be lame anyway?"

Sharkey and the others followed the bed to the door, and Sharkey called out to Conway, "Don't you worry, Jimmy boy. You may be a little shy in one leg, but mark my words, lad, you're going to take giant steps."

The door closed with a sharp snap. The head nurse was quite clearly not over her anger.

Sharkey continued, waiting until he was sure Conway was out of earshot. "You boys got yourself a real martyr for a friend. Make it work for you."

Patsy asked, "What're we gonna do with a martyr?"

"Times change. Prohibition ain't gonna last much longer. Take it from me. A lot more people are gonna be out of work."

Max looked over at Noodles; then, as if anxious to be convinced, he said to Sharkey, "Go on. We're interested."

"You ever think of setting yourselves up in business? You got plenty of cash you don't want the feds to know about. All those trucks they're using to haul liquor. They'll soon be selling them for nothing."

Noodles held up his hand. "Forget it. We're not interested in getting in the trucking business. It's a hard way to make a buck."

The phone rang and Sharkey picked it up, listened for a second, and then said, "Yeah, send him up." He put back the receiver and said, "A friend. You're thinking small, Noodles. I'm talking about hundreds of trucks, not just a few, controlled by a national organization and supported by a powerful union headed by our friend who's on his way to the operating room. Whatever you ask, there's no way he can turn you down. He owes you a lot—and you know too much about how that strike got turned around. Don't worry, he'll play ball."

16

Miami Beach was still a raw, unformed resort area. New, flashy hotels had sprung up, surrounded by swaying palms and freshly planted lawns. A few of the hotels had sparkling pools to go with their garish decor, but most of visitors preferred the white sand and deep-blue ocean, which patrons at a given hotel had at their disposal. The women wore skirted bathing suits that covered more of their anatomy than the men would have preferred, while the men were in tight trunks and striped undershirts that emphasized their physiques.

Near the garden of one of the hotels, just a

stone's throw from the beach, a newsboy had attracted quite a crowd with his loud but indistinct cries. The papers he held in his hand were selling like hotcakes, and as people read the headline, there were shouts of joy.

One bather tossed his paper high in the air, and while it stayed aloft for a moment on the ocean breeze, he fell to his knees as though in prayer and began to dig in the sand. Bringing forth a brown-tinted bottle that unmistakably held some potent sort of beverage, he raised the flask to the heavens in mock thanksgiving before he removed the top and began openly and brazenly to guzzle.

Eve, in a snazzy new bathing suit, bought a paper. She read as she moved up the beach to where Noodles, Max, and Carol lay stretched out on a huge beach towel. Noodles had his eyes closed and seemed to be asleep while Max and Carol, unmindful of the shocked frowns of the bathers nearby, were groping each other with tasteless familiarity.

Eve knelt beside Noodles and spread the newspaper over his face. Rousing himself out of a deep sleep, he smiled at Eve, held the paper away from his face, and read the headlines.

Without moving, his face a blank, he asked Max, "How much we got in the locker?"

Max, pulling his tongue out of Carol's mouth, asked, "Why? You wanna make a loan?"

Noodles handed him the paper. "Come Christmas we're unemployed."

Max and Carol looked at the headlines: VOLSTEAD ACT REPEALED. PROHIBITION TO END IN DECEMBER.

"Shit," Max said and then, answering Noodles, added, "About a million bucks, give or take."

"Jeez," Carol said, impressed, "Where do you keep it?"

His mood changed, Max answered nastily, "In my underwear."

"Oh, yeah? I woulda found it there long ago."

Max threw down the paper.

Noodles yawned and stretched. "We gotta reorganize, Max. I gotta couple of ideas."

Smoothing the sand in front of him, Max started to draw unintelligible designs. "Me, too."

"If I had a million, I'd take it easy," Eve said.

"We'll take it easy when we got twenty ... fifty ..." Max continued to finger the sand.

Noodles asked, "Where we gonna get it?"

"Right here." Max pointed to a spot on the drawing. Looking at it closely, Noodles could make out a crosswork that could have been streets and a square that might have represented a building.

"What's that?"

Distractedly, Max replied, "A dream . . ." He hit his fist against his forehead. "A dream I been dreaming for years. And I swear to God, Noodles, you and me are gonna make it come true. It'll be the biggest payday ever."

"What is it?"

Max looked up from the drawing and caught and held Noodles' gaze. "The Federal Reserve."

Noodles looked at Max incredulously. "Bank vaults underground a hundred feet or more, the whole place crawling with cops. You've got to be kidding."

"Noodles, my pal, my buddy, you ganef, Max Bercovicz never kids. Believe me, it's the longest step we can take. Remember, 'Take big steps, you get there faster.' "

"You're crazy."

Max's face went red. The veins in his temple stood out, throbbing violently, as he grabbed Noodles by the wrists and shouted into his face, "Don't ever say that to me, Noodles. Don't ever say that again."

*   *   *

In retrospect, it was all so clear, the pictures from the past. Noodles had it all set down in his memory, as though he'd written it in a journal. Crowning and Chicken Joe and Willie the Ape; Jimmy Conway, Sharkey, the union; Eve, Carol, the trip to Miami Beach. It had taken him time to piece it all together, starting with the day of the explosion, but now that he was back and had started to remember, everything was falling into place. Oh, there were a couple of pieces to the puzzle he hadn't figured out yet, but he was getting there. It had taken time, all right, yet it seemed to him that he'd had help every step of the way, as though someone wanted him to succeed, to find out everything, and most of all wanted him to find out why he was here, back in New York, when all of them were dead. Well, almost all of them. Moe was still alive, and somewhere out in Hollywood Deborah was a big star. Everyone else was gone, though, unless you counted Conway. Everyone but himself and the woman he had come to see, he realized as he sat in the salon of the rest home waiting for her to speak.

Her face was lined, her hair gray-white, but it was unmistakably Carol. She fixed her haggard eyes on him. "Walk with me."

They got up and left the main room, passing the dining room, where a few people were still eating, only the clink of silver breaking the silence.

Without looking at him she began to talk, a touch of the old antagonism coming through in her voice. "So much has happened and so many are dead. How many years have you been waking up feeling guilty about killing Max?"

In the hallway Noodles stopped in front of a photograph that hung on the wall. It depicted some sort of festivities at the home, an inaugural party, perhaps. A group of elderly inmates were gathered behind a banquet table flanked by doctors, dignitaries, and all the bigwigs who contribute to such places. These important people clutched champagne bottles and glasses; some had raised their arms in a toast. In the center of the photo stood the star attraction, a beautiful and elegant middle-aged woman. Noodles recognized Deborah at once.

"What's this?" he asked.

"Opening night. Fifteen years ago. I wasn't here yet."

"And her?" He didn't have to point. She knew who he meant.

"The patron saint of the place. An actress."

"You know her?"

"No."

Suddenly Carol said, "Did you know his father was put away in the nuthouse? And Max's brain was rotting, too . . . if he wasn't crazy then, he woulda been soon."

As he left, Noodles mused on what she had said. Yes, it was all making sense, all of it, even his own part. He'd thought he knew what was going on, but all along the way he'd been outsmarted.

Sitting in the car, Noodles and Carol studied the outside of the Federal Reserve Bank in Lower Manhattan. It was an imposing building, massive, gray, solid, designed to give off an aura of respectability and surety. It was also well-guarded and seemingly impregnable. Carol switched off the ignition, and the two of them studied the bank, noticing that the streets seemed full of people, although it was during working hours.

Finally she took a drag on her cigarette and asked him, "What chance is there a crackpot scheme like this might work?"

"Ask Max. You're with him day and night. While you're humping him, ask him. Maybe he'll be so excited he'll let you know what I can't figure out."

"Look, Noodles, you and I have never been exactly kissing cousins except that one time in Detroit. We put up with each other because of Max. Well, this is one time we could really do something for him ... together. Then we can go back to hating each other's guts. Otherwise, it's suicide for you, too, as well as the others. Suicide, pure and simple."

"Then talk him out of it. You got your methods. What the hell do you think God put that thing between your legs for, except to use it to push some guy around?"

"I *had* my methods. And believe me, I know how to use 'that thing,' but we don't screw anymore. All he can do is talk about tear gas and hostages. He's going to go through with it, with you or without you." She flipped her cigarette away and looked over at Noodles. "If you went to jail first, there wouldn't be any bank job." She tried to gauge his reaction, but his face remained impassive. "Actually, it was Max's idea."

"How's that?"

"He laughs at you. He says Eve's cut your balls off. He says you wet your pants every time you walk past this place. He's just mouthing off, but he says you'd be happy if the cops nabbed you, for whatever reason, and kept you from doing the job. Is that true?"

His silence, as he stared at the bank, answered her question.

"Then, go on. Turn him in to the cops. Put

him in jail. At least till he comes to his senses. And if you can't stand being away from him, go in with him. You're better-off there than dead."

She started the engine. "You know what's right better than I do. But if you don't do it, Noodles, I will."

A little black coffin floated through the
darkness. On it was a scroll that read PROHI-
BITION. Four bottles of champagne, empties,
served as candlesticks. The coffin was being
borne on the shoulders of two waiters who
carried it across the main room of Fat Moe's
Speakeasy. A line of dancers, each with his
or her hands on the hips of the preceding
person, had formed. They moved behind the
coffin, swaying their hips rhythmically to
the wailing music of the jazz bad. The band
played a funeral march, the kind heard in
New Orleans when a famous black musician
was piped to his grave. The mourners sobbed,

most of them in a mocking fashion, but for some of them, bootleggers and owners of illegal bars, the sobbing was real. Their livelihood was gone. For the majority, however, this night was a time of joy. Liquor had become legal again.

Patsy, Cockeye, and Peggy were on the dance line, all of them tight from booze and excitement. Max, on the sidelines, his eyes bright with anticipation, watched the dancers as they snaked between the tables. Carol was by his side, nervous, anxious, watching his every move. More and more customers joined the line, laughing, drinking, tossing flowers. It was a special night, a night like no other, the wildest party ever, a night no one would be likely to forget.

Noodles, with Eve beside him, sat at the bar. The patrons' tomfoolery delighted her, and she hardly noticed that Noodles had grown morose, grim, and serious, as if sickened by the merriment. Several times she tried to engage him in conversation, to lighten him up, but finally, when nothing would help, she became worried.

"What's the matter? Aren't you having a good time?"

Noodles forced a smile, pulled out a pocket watch, checked the time, then emptied his glass with one swig.

"Why are you going out tonight?" she persisted. "Why bother now that Prohibition is almost over?"

"Everyone's selling out," he answered. He paused, thought about what he had said, and then went on. "They offered us whiskey for almost nothing, so I said we'd take it off their hands." He looked at her. "We'll be gone for a while."

"I'll be waiting at the hotel. I like it when you come home late and wake me up."

"I won't be home tonight." He paused. "Or tomorrow, either."

Aware of his seriousness, Eve tried to keep the worry out of her voice. "I thought you'd only be gone a couple of hours."

She would have questioned him further, but at that moment all the lights in the speakeasy came on, illuminating the coffin, which had been set up on a table in the back of the room. There was wild cheering and applause. Max detached himself from Carol, strode to the center of the room, and raised his arms, gesturing for silence.

"Ladies and gents—if there's any here. I drink to the death of Fat Moe's Speakeasy. I mean, who the hell would want to drink here legally?"

Everyone laughed while waiters popped corks and poured champagne all around.

There were toasts and kisses, and more champagne and more toasts and more kisses. Fat Moe, assisted by a couple of waiters, began to cut the coffin-cake, passing out pieces to anyone who wanted some. Seeing that the wake was in full swing, Max left the center of the revelry and moved to the bar, where Patsy and Cockeye stood waiting. He ordered a refill, then held his glass up to them in a private, intense, and emotional toast.

"Boys, let's drink to our last shipment, because there's more on board tonight than just booze. There's ten years of our lives. Ten years that were really worth living. I don't know what I woulda done without you two. I guess we're out of the booze business, but there's a lot of surprises still to come."

They drank, but the toast wasn't enough for Max, and he wrapped his arms emotionally around the two of them, almost hysterical in his affection. Letting go finally, he looked for Noodles, who was sitting at a nearby table.

"Noodles!" he called. Lifting his glass again, he said, *"L'chayim."* Noodles didn't move, but he did raise his glass to his lips, barely wetting them with the bubbly contents.

From the bar Carol watched the two of them closely, completely oblivious to the band, which had begun to play again at an even higher and more frantic pitch.

Eve, who was sitting at the table with Noodles, asked, "How long will I have to wait?"

Turning his eyes on her, he answered, "A year and a half, more or less. Six months off for good behavior." When she started to question him further, he interrupted. "Don't ask. You don't want to know anything. Remember that. You don't know nothin'. I don't confide in you, I tell you nothin'. Just keep saying that, no matter what." He got up and she reached her hand up to find his. He smiled down at her and said, "Eat. Sleep. And dress warm."

Withdrawing his hand, he left the table and crossed the room without looking at anyone. Carol watched him anxiously. Max, too, was studying him as Noodles walked into the office, shut the door, and turned the key in the lock. He went straight to the telephone and dialed a number. The sound of the ringing just aggravated his already-nervous condition. It seemed like a lifetime, a lifetime when, like a drowning man, all that he had done, all that he had been, passed before him.

Finally he heard a voice. "Twenty-third Precinct. Sergeant Halloran."

Noodles took a deep breath before he said, "I got a tip for you."

There was a knocking at the door. Noodles put the receiver back on the hook and, pale and tense, unlocked it, admitting Max.

"What's the matter?" Max asked. "You sick? It's a big night, partner, in more ways than one. You don't want to get sick, tonight of all nights. I'm depending on you."

"I'm fine," Noodles replied quietly.

"You don't look it. In fact, you look like shit. Hell, Noodles, maybe you'd better not come with us. It'll be okay. We'll manage."

"Why shouldn't I come? I'm fine, I told you."

Max put his foot up on the throne and began polishing his shoe with a silk handkerchief. "I've been watching you all night. All you been doin' is drinking. You got to get your courage up? Hey, maybe that's it. All that drinkin'. Maybe the rotgut we serve made you sick, huh?" Max's tone was light, but beneath his kidding ran a thread of concern.

When Noodles didn't answer, Max looked up from his polishing. "We're only bringin' in a shipment of booze, right? You got so even that scares you? Maybe you'd better stay home with Eve. Sit by the fire, she can knit, you can read the paper. Real cozy and safe, huh?"

"I'll go wherever you go, Max."

Max started on the other shoe, buffing it until it shone like a black mirror. "Maybe Sharkey was right, maybe I oughta dump you."

Turning away from him, Noodles said very deliberately, "You really are crazy."

Straightening up with a howl, Max screamed "Don't say that!" He leapt at Noodles and smashed him on the back of the neck. Stunned, Noodles started to fall; as he did so, he saw Max's face, twisted in rage, then Max's hand holding the muzzle of a gun, the butt end coming toward Noodles' face. Then everything went black.

He'd thought it all through; there was no more reason to delve into the past. Carol had given him the answers he needed—most of them, anyway. Now there was just one more person to see. That was why he was at the theater, watching Shakespeare's *Antony and Cleopatra*. So he could see Deborah—and talk to her.

Waiting outside her dressing room, he felt his throat constrict. Was it really worth it? Why did he have to find the answer to the riddle? He should follow Fat Moe's advice, take the money and run. The only trouble was, if he'd been found after all these years, he'd be found again. No, he had to play the game according to their rules, and see where it led him.

Backstage it was noisy, although the curtain had been down for some time. Stagehands were setting up for the next night's performance; actors were leaving in clusters, high from the experience of performing, loud and showing off for one another. Props were being moved into the wings by two men who almost knocked Noodles over in their haste to be done with the night's work; the only thing left on the stage was the royal throne. Looking at it reminded him of Max and his Romanian throne. So many years ago.

An elderly woman with gray hair dressed in a maid's uniform opened the dressing-room door and invited Noodles in. He nodded and followed her, his hands sweating.

He went through a small anteroom into a much larger one, the dressing room of a star. Standing in the middle of the room, without her crown and wig but still wearing her queenly robes and her makeup, was Deborah. Seen close up, the makeup was a heavy mask, created to preserve Cleopatra's tragic intensity for those unlucky enough to have seats far from the stage.

They looked at each other in a silence that was thick with tension. Noodles spoke first, gulping a little, trying to make his words sound light, to hide the depth of his feelings.

"Hello, Deborah. Aren't you going to say something?"

"What do you say after more than thirty years? Hello? How've you been? Long time no see?"

"Not bad. How about, 'How are you? You're looking good.' If that doesn't seem appropriate, how about 'I was hoping I'd never see you again.' "

Her voice was troubled when she answered. "I didn't *think* I'd ever see you again. There's a difference."

Scrutinizing her, weighing her words and actions, Noodles said, "At least you recognized me. That's something. After all these years."

"Actresses have good memories." Going to a table that held bottles, mixers, and an ice bucket, she asked, "Drink?"

"No. No, thanks."

"I'm having one." She poured herself a stiff one, her hand shaking. Taking a sip, she spoke to the maid, who was busy behind a large screen. "Margot, I don't need you for now."

Taking a costume in her arms, the maid

left quickly, saying, "All right, miss. I'll be down the hall."

"Miss?" Noodles asked. "You never got married?"

"No."

"You live alone?"

She hesitated for a second before she answered. "No."

Sitting at the dressing-room table, she put her glass down and began carefully to comb out her hair.

Noodles watched her in the mirror.

She asked, "Where were you?"

"Out of town."

"When did you get back?"

"A few days ago."

"Staying?"

"It depends."

She began to pin up her hair. "Why did you want to see me? For old times' sake?"

"Two reasons. First, to see if you'd done the right thing when you turned me down to become an actress."

"Well?"

"You did. You were terrific. Better than that. You were perfect. Magnificent. I can't really find the right words." Embarrassed, he looked away, only to find himself staring at a huge poster of her in her Cleopatra makeup. A few lines from the play were quoted underneath her face. "Age cannot wither her, nor custom stale her infinite variety."

"It's like it was written for you," he said. " 'Age cannot wither her . . .' "

There was a trace of a smile on her lips. "I've still got my makeup on. Believe me, Noodles, it makes a difference."

"No. No difference. You must have made a deal with the devil."

"Yes, but it's the other way around. I didn't trade my soul to keep my youth. I sold my youth for my soul." She brought the glass to her lips, took a long swig, and thus fortified, asked the question. "The other reason?"

It was a question she didn't want to ask. He knew it and kept her waiting before he told her.

"To decide whether or not I should go to a party tomorrow night."

Trying to appear casual, she asked, "A party?"

Equally casual, he replied, "Out on Long Island. Secretary Bailey's place."

Her hand stopped in midair, the glass seemingly frozen there. Having trouble keeping her voice steady, she said, "You know Secretary Bailey?"

"No. Funny thing, though. I got invited to his party. An out-of-towner, only in the city a few days, no friends, no contacts, yet I got an invitation. To a big shot's house."

"If you don't know each other, why did he invite you?"

"Funny. I thought you might know something about it."

"Me? Why?"

"Because you know him. Because I've been asking some questions and—" He was interrupted by a knock at the dressing-room door.

"Who is it?" Deborah called out, relieved at the interruption.

"It's me, Deborah—David. I came to get you. Can I come in?"

A note of panic was in her voice. "No! Not now. Just a minute. Wait outside. I'll ... I'll call you."

"Okay." There was a pause, and the voice added, "I'll be right here."

Noodles waited until she got control of herself before he asked, "What does Secretary Bailey want from me?"

"You came here to ask me that? How should I know? *Why* should I know? I'm not his social secretary."

His voice grew tough. "Why did he send me that invitation?"

All of a sudden, after a lifetime of practiced control, she lost it, and her voice rose hysterically. "I don't know! I don't know!

Why should I know anything about your invitation? What do you want from me? Why did you come here? I know nothing . . . nothing."

"I take it back. You're not such a hot actress. At least not all the time. Right now you're one lousy actress." His insult didn't have the desired result. When she didn't respond, he took a step forward, as though he might strike her; then he spoke again, his voice insistent. "Who is Secretary Bailey?"

Tonelessly she replied. "He's a big businessman. He came here as a poor immigrant and made a lot of money in San Francisco and L.A., where he's been living for more than thirty years—"

"Skip the bio. I already know that. It's in the newspapers. What else?"

"He married a wealthy woman who died after their son was born. A few years ago he went into politics and moved here."

"More bullshit from the newspapers. All past history. What about right now? Right this minute."

"Right now he's in trouble."

"You bet he is. By the way, why are you afraid to tell me you're his lover, that you've been living with him for fifteen years? Gossip-column stuff, Deborah, but it's in with the news clippings and recapped in every story."

The tension drained from her face. She turned away from Noodles, looking at her reflection in the mirror.

After studying herself she said, "Age *can* wither me, Noodles. We're both old. The only things left are some memories. If you go to that party, you'll lose those, too. Tear up that invitation. There's a back door behind that screen; it leads into the alley. Use it . . . get away from here, as far away as you can, and don't turn around, don't look back." Her eyes were pleading, but his were cold. "I'm begging you, Noodles."

"You afraid I might turn into a pillar of salt? 'Don't look back.' I told you I studied the Bible in prison. Well, are you afraid something will happen to me if I don't run away?" He heard his voice, raised, for the first time in their conversation.

She bowed her head, but her voice was hard and challenging. "If you go out that door, yes."

He shook his head as if he couldn't believe what she had become, then turned, and despite her pleading gesture, opened the door.

He stopped just as she had predicted, stood as motionless as Lot's wife, in her salty state, must have. There on the empty stage, sitting on Cleopatra's throne, was Max, the Max of thirty-five years ago, only this Max had shoulder-length blond hair. Deborah came up behind Noodles and put her hand lightly on his arm as though to reassure him—or perhaps hold him up.

The boy on the throne waved to her and grinned. Even the grin was Max's. Her voice no more than a whisper, Deborah performed the introduction.

"This is Secretary Bailey's son, Noodles. His name is David. The same as yours."

There was a long pause, then Noodles started to walk, moving past the boy, not looking back, across the blackened stage, out of their sight. The boy David looked at her, questioning. A single tear traced a path down her cheek.

18

Secretary Bailey stood at the window of his study on the second floor of his house on Long Island, scanning the spacious grounds that made up his domain. He could see his reflection in the glass pane and noted that he had grown older-looking in the past few months. Only his eyes, although anxious now, were still bright with excitement, much as they had been when as a young man named Max Bercovicz he had made his first million in booze and death.

There was a party going on below, a party that he had arranged. His last party, he told himself. Lanterns and flares lighted the elaborate walks, roadways, and gardens as well as the gravel path that led down to a wharf and the Long Island Sound. The grounds were already full of people, and more were arriving, sweeping up the long, curved driveway in elaborate limousines. Handsome women in smart couturier gowns, men in tuxedos, military officers in full bemedaled regalia. They all seemed to know one another, greeting fellow guests with formal handshakes, hand-kissing, and manly slaps on the shoulder.

Waiters circulated with wine, champagne, and trays of food; buffet tables with more of the same were scattered about the place, their lavish spreads testifying to the wealth and importance of the host. Hidden speakers carried tunes from the most fashionable society orchestra playing inside in the ballroom.

The elegance, the luxury, the sophistication, all were real; here all that glittered *was* gold. Everyone was circulating, mixing, talking, behaving as they should: with the conscious satisfaction of being very rich and very powerful. In one respect no one was more satisfied by this than the man who had brought this all to pass, Secretary Bailey— formerly, in another existence known to only a few of the partygoers, Max Bercovicz.

Max could see Deborah in the crowd, dazzling as ever, surrounded by admirers, hangers-on, and those people impressed by being in the presence of a big star who was also mistress to a powerful man.

Near her was David with a group of friends, younger and less secure than most of the guests, but already beginning to assume the mantle of success, most of them quite aware that they were to the manor born.

Then Max saw something that made him pull back from the window. Crossing the room to his desk, he went up to a bank of monitors, part of an internal television circuit. He snapped on the four screens and saw the same scene he saw from the window. He flipped a few switches so that the screens now gave him views of most of the entrances and byways of the household.

His study was a huge, dark room, oak-paneled, with gilt-bound books gleaming from the bookshelves; the windows were shrouded in heavy velvet; a priceless Chinese rug was on the floor; an original Old Master hung over the mantel. Affluence and luxury—the room spelled that out clearly.

An intercom buzzed and Max said into it, "Show him up." He turned his attention back to the monitors, watching as he saw

Noodles enter the living room, followed by one of the butlers. On the third screen, Max could see Noodles stop and look searchingly at David before he continued off the screen and back to the second monitor, where the butler, leading the way, brought him up the wide staircase.

Then Max saw Deborah, her face drawn, looking upward, her eyes anxiously following Noodles as he ascended. Once Max was sure Noodles was on his way, he got up from the desk and went back to the window. He stood there motionless, his back to the door, staring into the garden.

He could see his son, David, youthful and exuberant, joining a group of his friends, young people unaware of what was happening in the world. David ducked his head down and kissed an extremely pretty girl on the shoulder. Max smiled. Then David, as if he felt his father's gaze, looked up at the window and gave an affectionate wave.

Max waved back, a smile in his eyes, then his face turned tense and brooding as he heard the door open and the butler say, "Go right in, sir." The door closed. Max waited, still with his back to Noodles.

Finally, still without turning, he said, "What are you waiting for? Come on in."

"For what, Mr. Bailey?"

Max turned and looked at Noodles, who was still standing by the door. They gazed at each other over a span of thirty-five years. Finally Max smiled. "To have a seat, Noodles." Max gestured to a large leather armchair at the head of a dark mahogany conference table.

"Thanks." Noodles didn't sit, but stood in the center of the room, arms at his side, curious but strangely relaxed, as though he had finally come to his journey's end.

"I'm glad you accepted my invitation. I was afraid you might not be curious."

"I *was* curious. I've never seen so many important people close up. You must have a lot of friends."

"Rats usually desert a sinking ship. In my case, they're flocking on board, to a big party that is quite a bit like a wake, only there's no dead body laid out in the front parlor ... yet."

"Yeah, I read in the papers that you've got your troubles. But, then, when you climb to the top of the ladder, it's a long way down ... and when you get to the top, there are certain responsibilities and certain risks. It's not all gravy, is it?"

"No. I always figured it had to end sometime."

Max crossed to the bar and filled two

glasses with whiskey. Looking in the mirror, he saw Noodles reach his hand inside his jacket. Max froze, then relaxed when he saw Noodles bring out his invitation and hold it up.

"Why did you ask me to come to your party, Mr. Bailey?"

Max carried the drinks back and put one on the table in front of Noodles. His hands were sweating and he was beginning to feel uncomfortable. "The invitation doesn't mean a goddamn thing. All that counts is what was in that suitcase, the money and the contract."

"It didn't say who the contract was on," Noodles said.

"Haven't you figured it out?"

"You, Mr. Bailey?"

Max barely nodded.

"I haven't had a gun in my hand for many years. My eyes aren't what they used to be, even with my glasses. My hand shakes sometimes. I wouldn't want to miss, Mr. Bailey."

Flaring up, Max said, "Cut the comedy, Noodles. I called you. I got you here to even up the score. They're going to get rid of me before the hearing. Today's as good a day as any." He took a gun from the desk drawer and placed it on the table beside the drink. "You do it, Noodles. You're the only person

I can accept it from. And you've got it coming. To even things out, settle the score. For what I did to you. Not just the money, everything."

Max pointed to a small door set in the woodwork. "You can get out through there. It leads down the back stairs to the street. I had it put in for a clean getaway—for myself. Go ahead, do it. No one will see you leave. You got the money, you can go wherever you want, live like a king for however many years you got left."

"I don't know what you're talking about, Mr. Bailey. You don't owe me a thing."

Max looked at him incredulously, his voice a crescendo of grief and frustration. "Your eyes were too full of tears to see it wasn't me lying there burned up on the street; it was somebody else. And you were too shocked to realize that the cops were in on it, too. That was a syndicate operation, Noodles. And you were the number-one sucker."

Without expression, Noodles said, "You must be crazy, Mr. Bailey."

"You said that once before, Noodles. I was as sane then as I am now. I let you think I was crazy, you and Carol, to make it stick. Noodles, I took your life away from you; I've been living in your place. I took everything—your money, even your girl. I've been fucking her for fifteen years. All I left you was thirty-five years of grief over having killed me. So why don't you shoot me?"

Noodles looked down at the gun. Out of regret and nostalgia, images floated by, images from the past. Images from a time when everything seemed simple....

... There was Max, arriving on the overloaded wagon, the old-fashioned camera in his hand. Max, looking down at him, the two of them deciding whether to become friends or enemies....

... a big red balloon popping to the surface of the water of the bay. Excited, the two of them dancing in the boat until it tipped and they fell in the water....

... a corpse, disfigured beyond recognition, lying on the wet pavement. Blood everywhere; a cop pulling a sheet up, then tagging the toe. A huge mechanical street-cleaner washing the blood away, cleaning everything up as though it had never happened....

... a man on a throne ...

Lifting his gaze from the gun, Noodles said, "It's true I've killed people, Mr. Bailey. Sometimes I did it to defend myself; other times I was hired. A lot of people came to us: business rivals, partners, lovers. Sometimes we took the job, sometimes we didn't. It depended on a lot of circumstances. Yours is one we never would have touched, Mr. Bailey."

Dismay showed in his voice as well as on his face as Max asked, "Is this your way of getting revenge?"

"It's just the way I see things. I'm too old for revenge. The past is the past; nothing I could ever do would change it one bit."

After a long silence, Max opened a box on his desk, reached in, and took out an antique watch on a heavy gold chain, their first score, the beginning of their rivalry as well as their subsequent friendship. He showed it to Noodles, his old infantile arrogance coming to the fore.

"It's g:32, Uncle, and I've got nothing left to lose. When you've been betrayed by someone, especially by a friend, you hit back. Do it."

Shaking his head, Noodles went toward the door. "You see, Mr. Secretary, along with your story there's mine, and it's a lot shorter. Many years ago I had a friend. I turned him in to save him, but he preferred to die. He was a great friend. It went bad for him—and for me, too."

He opened the door, then turned back. "I hope the investigation turns out to be nothing. It'd be a shame if a lifetime of work was wasted. Good night, Mr. Bailey."

He went out, closing the door behind him.

Max was alone with his life, whatever brief amount of it was left.

He didn't hurry leaving the party. It wasn't that he wanted to hang around, but he knew Max would be watching him, at least for a few minutes on the monitors in the room, so Noodles wandered through the crowds until he found himself near the exit. There, standing idle on the street, was a garbage truck. It was an odd time to be collecting garbage, he thought. Walking by, he had the impression that there was someone sitting at the wheel. He could hear, somewhat in the distance, the sounds of the party, the laughter and the music growing fainter as he moved away.

A few feet farther along and he was engulfed in shadows. He stopped and turned around, confident that he couldn't be seen from the truck although he could see it quite clearly.

A man in evening dress was standing on the sidewalk, some distance from him. The man could have been Max, Noodles wasn't sure. The man started across the street, as though beckoned by the huge truck. As he disappeared from sight, there was a loud noise, and the truck motor suddenly drowned out the sounds of the party. With a shudder, it pulled away from the curb and started toward where Noodles stood hidden near a tree.

The tuxedoed man was nowhere in sight; it was as if he had been eliminated by the night, wiped out of existence. The truck came nearer, massive under the street lights. It passed Noodles and he looked after it, watching the great maw gape open and the meshed teeth grind upward in a slow, steady rhythm. Something black, perhaps the man in the tuxedo, was being swallowed up.

Then the vehicle was off in the distance, its reflectors glowing over the wheels like two fiery eyes, hellish in their intensity.

EPILOGUE

It was all over; he was released. He knew now what had happened, that he'd been used. Max *was* crazy. Not certifiably so, not destined to spend his life in the nuthouse the way his father had, but still, what he had done had not been the act of a sane man. But now Max was nothing more than garbage and the search was over. Noodles let his mind wander as he walked away from all the evil concentrated in the huge house on Long Island.

A car careened around a street corner, a vintage Ford, coming at him at full speed, its horn blaring. Jammed with loud, wild people, shouting and laughing, and waving as they drove past him, they screamed to him that Prohibition was dead. Their clothes, the hairdos, everything was from a different, earlier era. He shook his head, telling himself that he had to stop living in the past, that it was over.

Another car, this one a touring car with its top down, followed the Ford. It, too, was stuffed with merrymakers, revelers dressed in the garb of the thirties, waving whiskey bottles, drunk, screaming at him as though they would run him down, swerving down the street. Kids, he told himself, dolled up in clothes they'd found in the attic, going to a masquerade party of some sort.

A bottle flew through the air and smashed at his feet in an explosion of booze and shattering glass. Noodles could hear a crescendo of noise—music, horns, voices rising in a deafening roar. He took a few more steps, then turned the corner . . . and walked away from it all.

Exciting Fiction from SIGNET

(0451)

- [ ] **DOUBLE CROSS by Michael Barak.** (115473—$2.95)*
- [ ] **THE SEA GUERILLAS by Dean W. Ballenger.** (114132—$1.95)*
- [ ] **THE DELTA DECISION by Wilbur Smith.** (113357—$3.50)
- [ ] **HUNGRY AS THE SEA by Wilbur Smith.** (122186—$3.95)
- [ ] **THE LONG WALK by Richard Bachman.** (087542—$1.95)
- [ ] **NIGHT AND FOG (Resistance #1) by Gregory St. Germain.**
  (118278—$2.50)*
- [ ] **MAGYAR MASSACRE (Resistance #2) by Gregory St. Germain.**
  (118286—$2.50)*
- [ ] **SHADOWS OF DEATH (Resistance #3) by Gregory St. Germain.**
  (119991—$2.50)*
- [ ] **ROAD OF IRON (Resistance #4) by Gregory St. Germain.**
  (122313—$2.50)*
- [ ] **TARGET: SAHARA (Resistance #5) by Gregory St. Germain.**
  (126696—$2.50)*

*Prices slightly higher in Canada

Buy them at your local
bookstore or use coupon
on next page for ordering.

Exciting SIGNET Fiction For Your Library